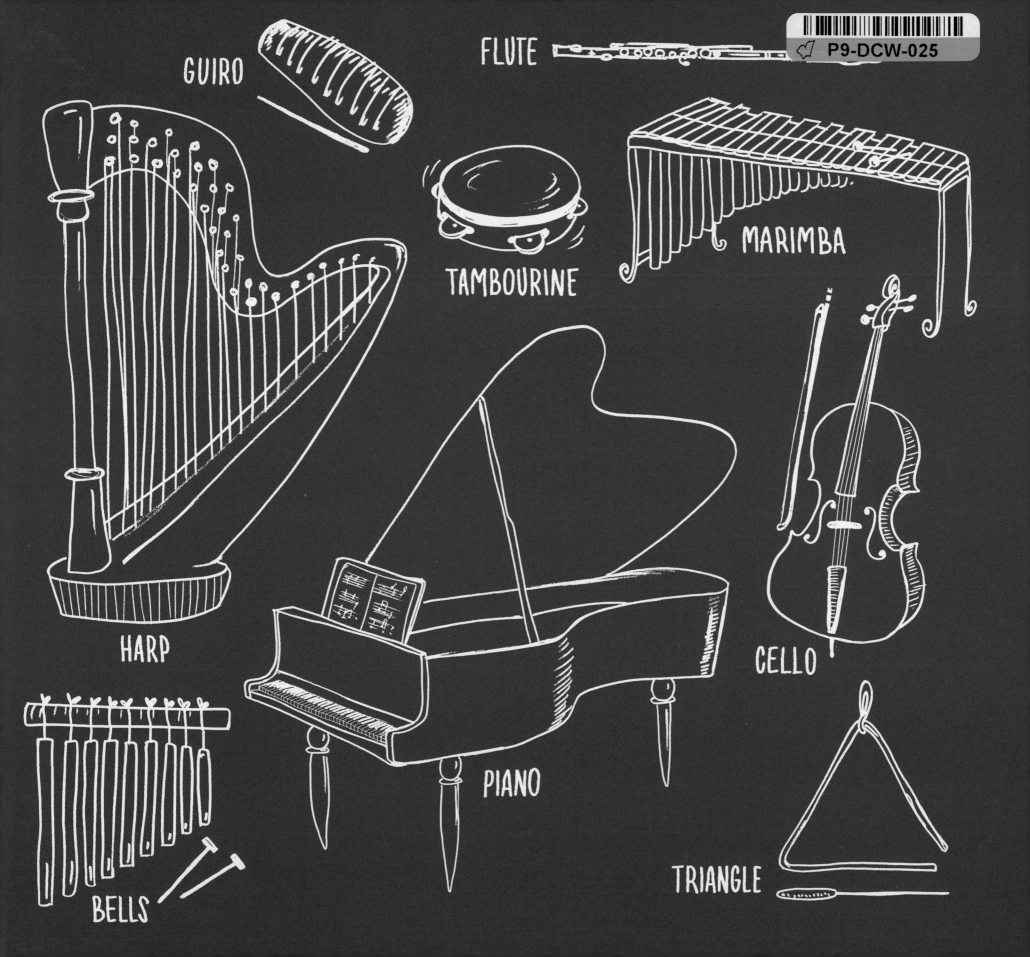

# A Secret Message from Maestro Mouse!

**PSSST!**

This is not a normal book.
You can LISTEN (not just look!).
If you want to, scan this square.
Music soon will fill the air.

*If you would like to hear music
while you read the book,
just scan this QR code to visit
wildsymphony.com
and download the free app.*

For my mom, who shared her love of music with me from the day I was born
—D.B.

For Robert, who taught me the loveliest melody of life
—S.B.

The author would like to express his gratitude to the entire *Wild Symphony* team, with special thanks to
Dani Valladares, Nicole de las Heras, Mallory Loehr, Barbara Marcus, Amy Bowman, Heide Lange, Bob Lord, and Susan Batori.

*Wild Symphony*
Dan Brown | Composer

Performed by the Zagreb Festival Orchestra

Bob Lord | Producer · Karl Blench | Orchestrator · Miran Vaupotić | Conductor · Jeff LeRoy | Audio Production Manager · Krešimir Seletković | Recording Producer ·
Jan Košulič | Lead Recording and Mixing Engineer · Tin Matijević | Orchestra Manager · Levi Brown | Recording Session Director · Lucas Paquette | Audio Director · Ivana Hauser | Orchestra Director ·
Emma Terrell | Assistant, Preproduction · Oliver Đorđević | Orchestra Coordinator · Gregory Brown | Musical Consultant · Marko Pletikosa | Videographer

Mastered by Adam Ayan at Gateway Mastering Studios

PARMA Recordings Production Staff:
Robert Leavitt · Janet Giovanniello · Sam Renshaw · Brett Picknell · Peter M. Solomon

Recorded at Blagoje Bersa Concert Hall, Academy of Music, University of Zagreb (Dalibor Cikojević, Dean)

**Violin I:** Sho Akamatsu | Concertmaster; Soloist, "Maestro Mouse Reprise" · Anton Kyrylov | Concertmaster; Soloist, "Eager Elephant" · Janez Podlesek | Concertmaster; Soloist, "The Ray," "Spider on a Web" ·
Marco Graziani | Concertmaster · Lana Adamović · Davide Albanese · Marija Bašić · Dunja Bontek · Marta Bratković · Ivana Čuljak · Žiga Faganel · Dana Kahriman · Saki Kodama · Teodora Sucala Matei · Marijan Modrušan ·
Barbara Polšek Sokolović · Vinka Fabris Stančec · Sergii Vilchynskyi · **Violin II:** Evgenia Epshtein | Soloist, "Spider on a Web" · Val Bakrač · Krešimir Bratković · Veronika Fišter · Tomislav Ištok · Vera Kurova · Mislav Pavlin ·
Leopold Stašić · Tanja Tortić · Branimir Vagroš · Kruno Vidović | Soloist, "Spider on a Web" · **Viola:** Lucija Brnadić | Soloist, "Spider on a Web" · Marija Andrejaš · Natalia Anikeeva · Marta Balenović · Nebojša Floreani · Aleksandar Jakopanec · Igor Košutić ·
Pavla Kovač · Jasna Simonović Mrčela · Tvrtko Pavlin · Magda Skaramuca · Tajana Škorić · Domagoj Ugrin · **Cello:** Branimir Pustički | Soloist, "Wondrous Whale," "Spider on a Web" · Adam Chelfi · Oliver Đorđević · Alja Mandič Faganel ·
Vanda Janković · Petra Kušan · Jurica Mrčela · Vinko Rucner · **Double Bass:** Helena Babić · Nikša Bobetko · Petar Brčarević · Borna Dejanović · Ivan Gazibara · Oleg Gourskii · Antal Papp · Marko Radić · Saša Špoljar · Jurica Štelma |
**Flutes & Piccolo:** Ana Batinica | Flute · Danijela Klarić Mimica | Flute, Alto Flute, Piccolo · Lucija Rašeljka Petrač | Flute, Alto Flute, Piccolo · Dijana Bistrović | Alto Flute, Piccolo · **Oboe & English Horn:**
Sanae Mizukami | Oboe · Vittoria Palumbo | Oboe · Iva Ledenko | Oboe, English Horn · Ema Abadžieva | English Horn · **Clarinet:** Dunja Paprić · Bruno Philipp · Marcelo Zelenčić · **Bass Clarinet:** Lovre Lučić · Danijel Martinović ·
**Bassoon & Contrabassoon:** Petar Križanić | Bassoon · Anita Magdalenić | Bassoon · Istvan Matay | Bassoon · Vasko Lukas | Bassoon, Contrabassoon · Damir Pulig | Contrabassoon · **Horn:** Yevhen Churikov · Bank Harkay ·
Viktor Kirčenkov · Antonio Pirrotta · Nikola Zver · **Trumpet:** Ivan Đuzel | Soloist, "Anxious Ostrich" · Mario Lončar | Soloist, "Anxious Ostrich" · Tomica Rukljić · **Trombone:** Zvonimir Marković · Ivan Mučić · Bruno Petak ·
Marin Rabadan · **Tuba:** Željko Kertez | Soloist, "Happy Hippo" · **Timpani & Percussion:** Krunoslav Benko | Percussion, Woodblocks Soloist, "Impatient Ponies" · Tomislav Kovačić | Percussion, Timpani Soloist, "Bouncing
Kangaroo" · Leonardo Losciale | Percussion, Crotales Soloist, "The Ray" · Hrvoje Sekovanić | Percussion, Timpani · Luis Camacho Montealegre | Percussion · Renato Palatinuš | Percussion · Fran Krsto Šercar | Percussion |
**Harp:** Milica Pašić | Soloist, "Spider on a Web" · Mirjana Krišković · Hana Paraušić | **Piano & Celeste:** Ljudmila Šumarova | Prepared Piano Soloist, "The Armadillo's Shell"

Visit us on the Web! rhcbooks.com
Educators and librarians, for a variety of teaching tools, visit us at RHTeachersLibrarians.com

Library of Congress Cataloging-in-Publication Data is available upon request.
ISBN 978-0-593-12384-3 (hardcover) — ISBN 978-0-593-12385-0 (glb)
Jacket art and interior illustrations by Susan Batori
The artist used Photoshop to create the illustrations for this book.
The text of this book is set in 13.5-point Tribute Roman.
Book design by Nicole de las Heras
MANUFACTURED IN CHINA
10 9 8 7 6 5 4 3 2 1
First American Edition

# DAN BROWN
# WILD SYMPHONY

*illustrated by* **Susan Batori**

## MAESTRO MOUSE

I'm Maestro Mouse. I'll be your guide.
So come along on my wild ride!

You'll meet my friends; they're smart and fun.
I think you'll love them—every one!

They live in jungles, ponds, and trees,
Out in fields and under seas.

Each one teaches something new,
A secret lesson just for you.

My friends and I, we have a plan—
Try to guess it if you can!

Listen well and use your eyes.
I think you'll love our big surprise!

I'll hide some clues along the way,
A hidden game—come on, *let's play!*

## WOODBIRD WELCOME

As the sunrise starts to glow,
Woodland birds all say hello.
Honking, hooting, chirping, peeping,
Squawking, tweeting, cooing, cheeping.
It's so noisy—all those birds!
A jumbled rush of birdly words!
But if you pause for not so long,
You'll hear each bird's own special song.

EVEN WHEN LIFE SEEMS MESSY, THERE'S BEAUTY TO BE FOUND EVERYWHERE.

## BOUNCING KANGAROO

Kanga kanga kanga roo,
Teach me how to bounce like you.
Bouncing high, bouncing low,
Bouncing everywhere you go!
Bounce to run—Ka-boing! Ka-boing!
Bounce for fun—Ka-foing! Ka-foing!
Bounce and eat—Ka-chew! Ka-chew!
Bounce asleep—Ka-snooze! Ka-snooze!
When you shake your kanga-tail
And bounce along the kanga-trail,
I wish, I wish I bounced like you.
I want to be a kanga-too!

IT'S GREAT TO ADMIRE THE SKILLS OF OTHERS, BUT DON'T FORGET THAT YOU HAVE SPECIAL TALENTS TOO.

## CLUMSY KITTENS

Jumping here, landing there,
Tabletop to kitchen chair.
Tree to fence to porch to roof.
Floor to couch to stool to— Oof!
Even though they sometimes fall,
They don't seem to mind at all.
Always landing on their feet,
Never crying in defeat,
When life trips them up a bit,
Cats just make the best of it.

FALLING DOWN IS PART OF LIFE.
THE BEST THING TO DO
IS GET BACK ON YOUR FEET!

## THE RAY

Hammerhead and moray eel
Loudly tell you how they feel.
But the fish just stare and sigh
When the ray goes gliding by.
Strong and graceful, silent too,
Could the ray be just like you?

SOMETIMES A LOT OF NOISE IS NOT THE BEST WAY TO GET ATTENTION. BEING QUIET AND GRACEFUL CAN WORK EVEN BETTER.

## HAPPY HIPPO

The hippo loves a muddy pond
With clumps of weeds to nibble on.
He's happy just to float and munch—
He's got his home, he's got his lunch.
He doesn't wish he had the sky.
Life's too short to moan and cry.
He just wants to splash and sing—
Life is such a simple thing!

SOMETIMES YOU GET SO CAUGHT UP IN THE CONFUSING PARTS OF LIFE THAT YOU FORGET TO ENJOY THE SMALL THINGS.

# FROGS IN A BOG

Croakers, peepers, happy frogs
Sing together in the bogs.
Big ones, small ones, fat ones too,
Green and brown and even blue.
No one's right and no one's wrong.
Everyone just sings along.

ALL OF US ARE DIFFERENT SIZES, SHAPES, AND COLORS. IF WE WORK TOGETHER WE CAN MAKE WONDERFUL MUSIC.

## ANXIOUS OSTRICH

When she's stressed or feeling hurt,
She sticks her head down in the dirt.
Here she finds a peaceful space
And doesn't feel so out of place.
But soon her hiding trick must end
(To eat her lunch or see a friend).
And once she's spent some time away,
She feels recharged to face the day!

WHEN YOU FEEL OVERWHELMED,
IT'S OKAY TO TAKE TIME FOR YOURSELF.

## THE ARMADILLO'S SHELL

An armadillo is really smart.
He's got a shell; he's got a heart.
He's got his shell when days are bad,
To keep out things that make him sad.
But when his days are really good,
He opens up just like he should.
He's not afraid to show his heart—
That's the way that friendships start.

IT'S OKAY TO BLOCK OUT BAD THINGS,
BUT DON'T FORGET TO OPEN UP
AND INVITE THE GOOD THINGS IN.

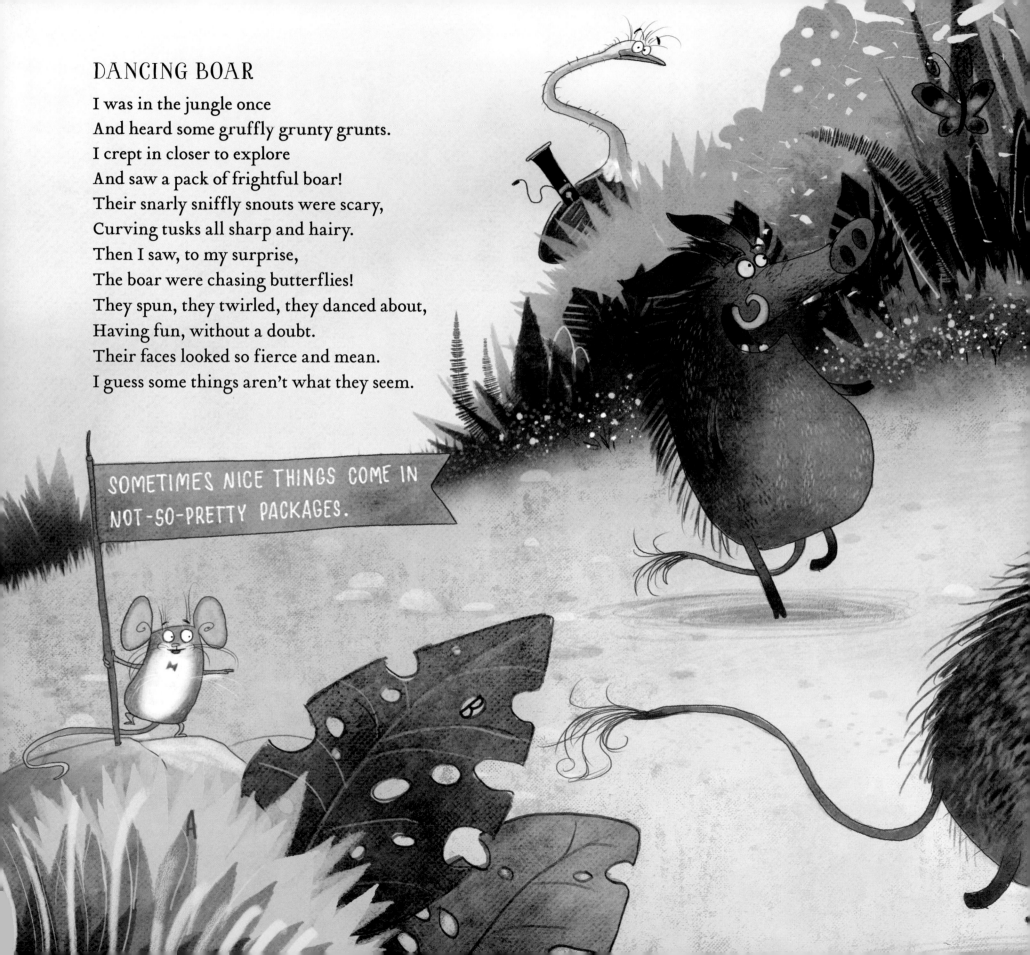

# DANCING BOAR

I was in the jungle once
And heard some gruffly grunty grunts.
I crept in closer to explore
And saw a pack of frightful boar!
Their snarly sniffly snouts were scary,
Curving tusks all sharp and hairy.
Then I saw, to my surprise,
The boar were chasing butterflies!
They spun, they twirled, they danced about,
Having fun, without a doubt.
Their faces looked so fierce and mean.
I guess some things aren't what they seem.

SOMETIMES NICE THINGS COME IN NOT-SO-PRETTY PACKAGES.

## IMPATIENT PONIES

Love to gallop, never trot,
Hate to stay in just one spot.
Running circles, life's a race,
Got to set a faster pace!
Looking forward, never down,
Missing clovers on the ground.
As tomorrow comes your way,
Don't forget to live today!

TOMORROW WILL BE SOON ENOUGH.
SLOW DOWN AND ENJOY TODAY!

## WONDROUS WHALE

The biggest creature of them all
Isn't hairy, mean, or tall.
He's sleek and kind and soft and blue,
Long and smooth and gentle too.
A hundred feet from mouth to tail,
Yes, you guessed—a big blue whale.
A whale can do a wondrous thing
Underwater—he can sing!
It's how he talks to other whales
And shares with them his whaley tales.
His voice can echo through the sea,
Two hundred miles (and sometimes three!).
So if you ever take a swim
And dare to stick your head way in,
You just might hear a distant song,
A whale who hopes you'll sing along!

IF YOU LISTEN CAREFULLY TO NATURE,
YOU'LL HEAR CONVERSATIONS
ALL AROUND YOU.

## CHEETAH CHASE

You can't see her, creeping low,
Inching forward . . . slow . . . slow . . . slow.
Even when you squint and stare,
You see nothing . . . nothing's there.
Then WHOOSH! A flash of yellow fur!
A streaking blaze! A cheetah blur!
In a heartbeat, she can shift
From super-slow to super-SWIFT!
But when a cheetah runs so fast,
Her cheetah speed will never last.
And so she stops to breathe and rest.
(A baobab tree for naps is best.)
She gives a yawn . . . and then a snore.
And then PAWOOSH! She runs some more!

IT'S IMPORTANT TO GIVE EVERYTHING YOU'VE GOT! BUT DON'T FORGET TO REST AND REFILL YOUR TANK.

## EAGER ELEPHANT

Ta ta-da! Ta ta-dee!
Practice singing just like me.
Yes, it's hard, but she won't quit.
Soon she'll get the hang of it!
Momma teaches, baby learns,
Brother giggles in the ferns.
Then at last she gets it right!
Ta ta-da! They'll dance all night!

## RAT ATTACK!

You run and hide when rats are near,
Dash away and shake in fear.
But if you stop and think a bit,
You'll see it should be opposite.
You're bigger, louder, smarter too.
The rat should run away—not you!

SOMETIMES WE'RE AFRAID OF THE SILLIEST THINGS!

THERE'S TIME FOR WORK,
AND THERE'S TIME FOR PLAY.
THERE'S TIME FOR BOTH EVERY DAY!

## BUSY BEETLES

Busy beetles, busy beetles,
Digging with their little feetles.
Working slowly as a turtle,
Building homes in garden dirtle.
But the beetles, bit by bittle,
Keep on going, never quittle.
When at last their work is done,
Then it's time to have some fun!

## SPIDER ON A WEB

In the woods you stop and shriek.
There's something sticky on your cheek.
A spider's web you almost broke,
Blech! Oh, yuck! You gasp and choke.
But as you start to run away,
There's something there that makes you stay.
Diamonds somehow caught in flight,
Hanging in the bright moonlight.
A shining net of silver-gray.
Who thought you'd see a web that way?
A masterpiece some spider spun—
Now aren't you glad you didn't run?

THERE'S BEAUTY IN
UNEXPECTED PLACES.
KEEP YOUR EYES OPEN—
YOU MIGHT BE SURPRISED.

## BRILLIANT BAT

Even though a bat can't see,
He never flies into a tree.
He never smacks into your house.
He's more than just a flying mouse.
He has no sight but has no fears
Because he knows how well he hears.
He doesn't really need to see.
He's learned to listen carefully.

BEING A GOOD LISTENER WILL
ALWAYS HELP YOU FIND YOUR WAY.

## SWAN IN THE MIST

In the mist I see a swan
By herself; her friends are gone.
She must be sad there all alone,
Paddling softly on her own.
But then I see she's got a smile.
She wants to be alone awhile.
Time to think and time to rest,
She likes this special time the best.

TIME WITH FAMILY
AND FRIENDS IS FUN.
TIME ALONE CAN BE SPECIAL TOO.

## CRICKET LULLABY

There are times when we just look
(Like when we read a picture book).
But if we use our ears to spy,
There's more to life than meets the eye.
At night a field looks dark and bare.
Our eyes are certain nothing's there.
But ears hear things that eyes can pass—
Our ears hear crickets in the grass.

NOW AND THEN,
CLOSE YOUR EYES AND LISTEN.
YOU MIGHT "SEE" SOMETHING NEW.

Dear Readers,

Long before I wrote stories . . . I wrote music.

My parents were both musicians and teachers, and I grew up practicing classical piano, singing in choirs, and attending LOTS of concerts. Music was a secret sanctuary for me as a child. It calmed me when I felt frustrated, was a trusted friend when I felt lonely, helped me express my joy when I was happy, and, best of all, sparked my creativity and imagination. Even now, I play piano every day— usually after I finish a long day of writing.

Music is a kind of storytelling, and the orchestral movements in *Wild Symphony*—combined with their accompanying poems and illustrations—all work together (like a code, of sorts!) to tell a story and reveal a funny or interesting side of an animal's personality. If you listen carefully, you might be able to find each animal hiding in the music. Even better, every animal in this book will share with you a simple moral . . . a fun collection of "secrets to life" that will help you on your way.

I hope you have as much fun experiencing *Wild Symphony* as I had creating it.

Sincerely,

D.B. age 3

ꟻLLꟿꟐ ᐸVᴧLᐸ VꟐOLꟐ ꟻᐸꟐꟐ LOVꟐO

TAP
TAP
TAP

In case you missed it, don't forget that you can
GO WILD with the free *Wild Symphony* music app!
Scan this QR code for the app, or visit wildsymphony.com,
where there are answers to the puzzles and much more!

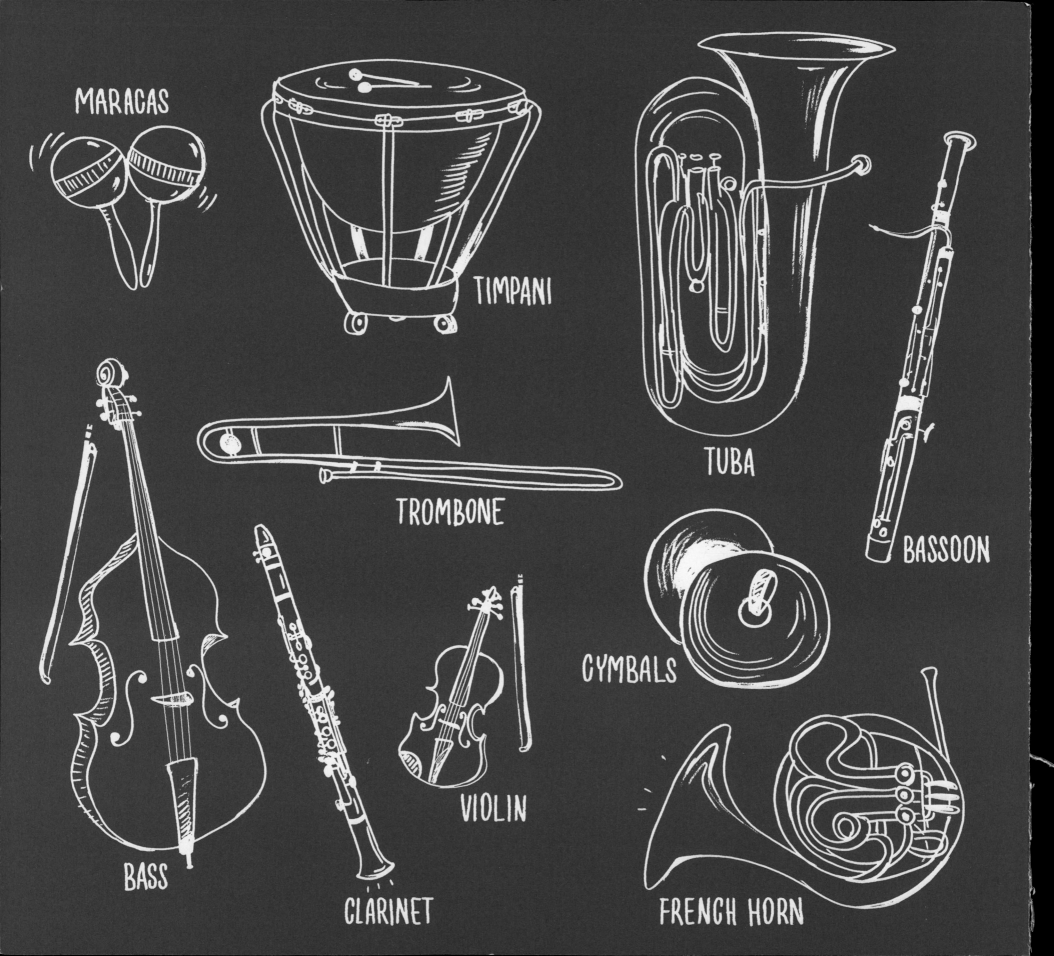

## WAR VIEWS.

Grand Review of the Great Veteran Armies of Grant and Sherman at Washington,
on the 23d and 24th May, 1865.
*Instantaneous*

Army of the Potomac. Looking up Pennsylvania Avenue from the Treasury Buildings,
Maj. Gen. Wright and Staff, and 6th Army Corps passing in Review.

No. 3392

PUBLISHED BY E. & H. T. ANTHONY & CO.,
American and Foreign Stereoscopic Emporium, 591 Broadway, New--York.
Negative by Brady & Co Washington.

---

## PHOTOGRAPHIC INCIDENTS OF THE WAR.

### No. 571.

IEW ON BATTLE FIELD OF ANTIETAM NEAR SHERRICK'S HOUSE, WHERE
THE 79TH NEW YORK VOLUNTEERS FOUGHT AFTER THEY CROSSED
THE CREEK. GROUP OF DEAD CONFEDERATES.

From
Gardner's Gallery, corner of 7th and D streets,
Washington, D C.

Negative by Alex. Gardner.

E. & H. T. ANTHONY, 591 Broadway, New York, Wholesale Agents.

*Surgeon Generals Office.*
*A. M. M.*

---

## 1861    The War for the Union.    1865

### PHOTOGRAPHIC HISTORY.

This series of pictures are *original photographs* taken during the war
of the Rebellion. A quarter of a century has passed away since the sun
painted these real scenes of the great war, and the "negatives" have
undergone chemical changes which makes it slow and difficult work to
get "prints" from them. Of course no more "negatives" can be made,
as the scenes represented by this series of war views have passed away
forever. The great value of these pictures is apparent. Some "negatives" are entirely past printing from, and all of them are very slow
printers.

### A WORD AS TO PRICES.

A gentleman living near Watkins' Glen, New York, wrote us that
he thought twenty-five cents each, too high a price for the stereoscopic
war views, as he could buy views of Watkins' Glen for $1.50 per dozen.
We wrote him to this effect; if there was but one negative of Watkins'
Glen in existence, and if Watkins' Glen itself was entirely wiped off the
face of the earth, and if this one negative was old and "dense" and very
slow to "print," and if all the people of this country were as much
interested in a view of Watkins' Glen as they are in seeing the real
scenes of our great war, so faithfully reproduced, *then, and only under
such circumstances*, should Watkins' Glen Pictures be compared to photographs made "at the front" during the days of 1861 to 1865. The
gentleman "acknowledged the corn," took the war views he wished for,
paid the reasonable price asked for them, and was satisfied.

The above is the only answer we shall ever make to the question of
*price*. We deem it necessary to say this much, as many persons write
and ask us for *cheap* war views; when we change the price of these war
views, it will be to double it; they will never be any cheaper than now.
They can be obtained only of

TAYLOR & HUNTINGTON, Publishers,

*Copyrighted.*                    No. 2 State Street, HARTFORD, CONN.

---

## 1861.    WAR VIEWS.    1865.

### No. 2611.

Dutch Gap Canal. Soldiers at work inside the dam. The mist arising against the bank is
caused by a rebel shell, which exploded just as this view was being photographed, December,
1864.

CW-460B

These are the *original* views taken by "Brady," the Government Artist, during 1861-2-3-4-5.
They can be obtained only of JOHN C. TAYLOR, 17 Allen Place, Hartford, Conn.
[Copyrighted.]

Anthony #2611

# The Civil War in Depth

# THE CIV
# IN DI

CHRONICLE BOOKS
SAN FRANCISCO

# VIL WAR
# EPTH

## History in 3-D

by Bob Zeller

Printed in Singapore.

Library of Congress Cataloging-in-Publication Data:
Zeller, Bob, 1952–
  The Civil War in depth: history in 3-D/by Bob Zeller.
   p. cm.
  Includes bibliographical references and index.
  ISBN 0-8118-1348-7 (hardcover)
  1. United States—History—Civil War, 1861–1865—Pictorial works.
   2. Photography, Stereoscopic. I. Title.
  E468.7.Z45 1997
  973.7-dc21               96-37387
                       CIP

Designed by Friedrich Design/Pete Friedrich, *Union*
and Yerkey Design/Jeff Yerkey, *Confederate (to the bitter end)*

The right-hand image of the stereo view on page 67 is reprinted from
*The Photographic History of the Civil War*, Francis T. Miller, ed.
[New York: Review of Reviews Co., 1911].

Distributed in Canada by Raincoast Books
8680 Cambie Street
Vancouver, British Columbia V6P 6M9

10 9 8 7 6 5 4 3 2

Chronicle Books
85 Second Street
San Francisco, California 94105

Web Site: www.chronbooks.com

## ACKNOWLEDGMENTS

Lee had Jackson, and for this project I had George Whiteley IV. His superb eye and skillful judgment are reflected on every page of this book. He photographed most of the stereo views, assisted in their selection, edited the manuscript, and offered articulate opinions on countless issues.

I owe a deep debt of gratitude to the private collectors and institutions listed on the picture credits page. They provided most of the views. There would be no book without their willingness to share from their collections. Special thanks to William A. Frassanito, who ignited my passion for Civil War photography and has generously shared his expertise; D. Mark Katz, who got me started as a collector; Brian Pohanka, who provided expert advice and editing assistance; Len Rosa of War Between the States Memorabilia; and my agent, Sally McMillan.

Thanks also to Mary Ison, Eva D. Shade, and Stephen Ostrow at the Library of Congress; Randy W. Hackenburg at the U.S. Army Military History Institute; Annmarie Price at the Virginia Historical Society; Dr. Wilbur Meneray and Courtney Page at Tulane University; Chris Hoolihan at the University of Rochester Medical School's Miner Library; Teresa Roane at the Valentine Museum; Elizabeth P. Bilderback at the South Caroliniana Library; Janice Madhu at the International Museum of Photography; Corinne P. Hudgins at the Museum of the Confederacy; Ann Sindelar at the Western Reserve Historical Society; Harris J. Andrews at Time-Life Books; John Dennis, editor of the National Stereoscopic Association's *Stereo World*, and Raymond and Majorie Holstein, caretakers of the NSA's Oliver Wendell Holmes Library at Eastern College in St. Davids, Pennsylvania; Brooks Johnson at the Chrysler Museum in Norfolk, Virginia; and Alison Devine Nordstrom at the Southeast Museum of Photography in Daytona Beach, Florida.

I also wish to thank Sal Alberti, Wm. B. Becker, David Belcher, John Beshears, Marden Blackledge, Sue Boardman, Greg Bobotis, Bob Boquette, Ken Budzek, James Curtin, John R. deTreville, Michael DiPrima, Michael D'Orso, Fields of Glory, Peter H. Fowler, Bryan W. Ginns, Nicholas and Marilyn Graver, Rob and Elizabeth Gibson, Bryan Ginns, Thomas Harris, James Hendry, James F. Henthorne, Ed Hinton, The Horse Soldier, Les Jones, Larry Kasperek, Cliff and Michelle Krainik, Jeffrey Kraus, Bruce Kusrow, Ron Labbe, Jules A. Martino, Tim McIntyre, Greg McMahon, John Pannick at Sword and Saber, Jordan Patkin, George Polakoff, E. Marshall Pywell, Jack C. Ramsay Jr., Harry Roach, Harvey Teal, Frank Watters, Forrest Wheeler, and Larry West.

*This book is dedicated to Ann, Sara, and Jesse Zeller and to my mother, Ruth Walker Zeller.*

# CONTENTS

7 | Picture Credits

9 | Foreword

13 | Introduction

20 | A Rebel Coup at Fort Sumter

26 | The First Year

36 | The Bloodiest Day

46 | Abraham Lincoln: A Man for the Ages

56 | Gettysburg

64 | A Sense of Action

74 | The Panorama of War

82 | Grant Takes Over

90 | The Art of the Stereo Photographer

96 | Sherman Captures Atlanta

102 | Petersburg and the Fall of Richmond

110 | The End of the War

118 | Bibliography

119 | Index

## PICTURE CREDITS

No. 239.   Interior of Fort Sumpter, looking toward Charleston.

# This is the first 3-D photographic history of the Civil War. Almost a book a week has been published about the war since it ended

132 years ago. But never has one been published about the stereoscopic photographs that so vividly brought the war into the parlors and living rooms of nineteenth-century America.

Many of the Civil War's finest and most recognizable images are 3-D photos, from M. B. Brady's image of three Rebel prisoners at Gettysburg to the hanging of the Lincoln conspirators by Alexander Gardner. Civil War enthusiasts, by and large, are only vaguely aware of the stereo photographer's role in the war. Photography is one of the least understood and most overlooked facets of the war, despite the fact that it is universally recognized as a foundation for our intense interest in that period of American history.

It is without cliché to say that the bare images themselves are the best evidence we have of what happened from 1861 to 1865. Those who embark on a study of the history of war photography invariably must tiptoe through a minefield of misinformation and inaccurate history. Remarkably little, in fact, is known about the photographers themselves. Even the most basic information eludes us about the most

*A Civil War Photographer at Work*
*When it was all over, the signature image of Civil War photography was made where it all began. Boston photographer John P. Soule aimed his camera across the battered remains of Fort Sumter and caught photographer Sam Cooley at work on the far parapet in 1865.*

famous war photographer of them all, M. B. Brady. Today, more than one hundred years after his death, we do not know when Brady was born. Was it 1823? Or 1824? We do not know how he spelled his first name. Was it Mathew? Or Matthew? He never left a clue, always signing "M. B. Brady." Were it not for the enterprise of an old Civil War correspondent in 1891, we would have almost nothing about Brady's life in his own words. George Alfred Townsend's interview of the aging photographer, published in the *New York World*, is the most comprehensive first-person record of Brady's life.

With this background, it is not surprising that the stereoscopic photo history of the war could, with time, fade from the public's consciousness and slip into obscurity. But the confusion and mystery surrounding Civil War photography provide an endlessly fascinating wellspring of opportunity for scholars and collectors.

The impeccably meticulous research of William A. Frassanito, the dean of Civil War photo historians, has led to four brilliant books and countless revelations and discoveries, particularly about the photographs of Gettysburg and Antietam. Frassanito is responsible for untangling much of the confusion and misinformation about war photos.

Inspired by Frassanito, photohistorian D. Mark Katz, and others, I began collecting and studying Civil War photographs in 1980. Much to my surprise, I discovered that unknown Civil War photos, both in 3-D and non 3-D, are still frequently uncovered, and that it is only a matter of time before someone discovers another fascinating new window into the most traumatic period of our country's history.

Nearly all of the photos in this book are published here for the first time as the photographers intended them to be seen—in full stereo. But at least a dozen images are published here, to the best of my knowledge, for the first time in any format, including one of the only known photographs of Civil War photos for sale during the war.

While the history of Civil War photography is riddled with gaps and littered with misinformation, there is an unmistakable theme of accomplishment as well. From the beginning to the end of the war, photographers in both the North and South eagerly sought new photographic opportunities and, as a result, attained ever-higher levels of photojournalistic achievement, usually using their stereo cameras.

Confederate stereo photos are exceedingly rare. The first war photographs, nonetheless, were taken by Southern photographers who took their cameras to Fort Sumter after its capture in April 1861. The most extensive series of these images—approximately thirty-five views in and around Fort Sumter and Fort Moultrie—are in the Tulane University Library. Some

of the best are featured in this book.

Few people know it, but nearly a quarter of the 130 known photographs of Abraham Lincoln were stereo images. Most were never marketed in the stereo format and were never intended to be viewed in 3-D. But after fifty-nine years of passionate collecting and careful research, artist Lloyd Ostendorf has reassembled nearly every Lincoln photo that can be seen in three dimensions. Some of the best in his collection are featured in this book.

Contrary to popular belief, there *were* action photographs taken during the Civil War. There are at least three, and they were taken in Fort Sumter on September 8, 1863, by a Southern photographer, George S. Cook. His accomplishment is now largely overlooked, but it was celebrated at the time by newspapers and by Cook's contemporaries. This is the first book to devote a chapter to the examination of Civil War action photography, including the photographs that made Cook the world's first combat photographer. Reproduced here is not only Cook's noted exploding shell photo, but his extraordinary images from the parapet of Fort Sumter that show Union gunboats shelling Fort Moultrie. *The Civil War in Depth* reveals for the first time that Cook actually made not one, but two photographs while under fire on Sumter's parapet. And it shows how Cook purposely moved his camera between exposures to create a makeshift 3-D photo with two separate exposures.

Most of the photos in this book were made from

## CIVIL WAR PHOTOS FOR SALE

This previously unpublished 1864 photograph is a rare image of photographic prints for sale during the war. It shows Philadelphia photographer Frederick Gutekunst's booth at the city's Great Sanitary Fair, a benefit for the U.S. Sanitary Commission and its work with wounded soldiers. Gutekunst photographed Gettysburg three weeks after the battle.

the original stereo views provided by private collectors. Some collectors were extraordinarily generous. John Waldsmith, author of *Stereo Views: An Illustrated Price Guide,* contributed four obscure, unpublished views. Michael Griffith lent two extraordinarily rare unpublished views of freed slaves on a South Carolina plantation. From his vast Lincoln collection, Lloyd Ostendorf contributed an unpublished photograph of Lincoln's first inaugural parade. Matthew R. Isenburg contributed one of the very few known stereo daguerreotypes of an American city scene—a recently discovered 1850s image of San Francisco. And Harris J. Andrews of Time-Life Books, one of the great unsung experts on Civil War photography, was kind enough to tell me of three spectacular, unpublished stereo views hidden in the vast collection of the Western Reserve Historical Society in Cleveland, Ohio.

Here, then, is Civil War photography the way it was meant to be seen—in full three dimension, with depth and detail that simply cannot be duplicated by a two-dimensional print. This is not a definitive history, but it is a start. In years to come, as Civil War scholars and enthusiasts exhaust the resources of the more traditional areas of study, perhaps more will turn their attention to the history of the war's photography and will fill more gaps in our knowledge of a subject that has been too often taken for granted.

# American photojournalism came

of age during the Civil War, just as television news found its place during the Vietnam War. The Civil War was the first war to be extensively photographed from start to finish, and Americans still are captivated by the conflict in large measure because of the many thousands of war photographs. But the great hidden fact about Civil War photography is that many of the images were made to be seen in three dimensions. Scores of the war's most enduring photographs were made by photographers who visualized the scenes in 3-D. These photographers aggressively marketed their images to enthusiastic purchasers, who paid as much as fifty cents apiece—one-third of a laborer's daily wage—for war views.

As it turned out, the stereo views were so historic, they still had tremendous impact when seen as single photographs in a two-dimensional format. Consequently, the pictures in every photographic history of the war before now have been published in two dimensions, and that is typically how we have come to see them. But our ancestors knew something that has been largely lost to us. They knew that many of the great photos of the war were designed to be seen not merely with the naked eye but through the convergent lenses of a stereoscope.

The stereoscopic viewer is a strange-looking, handheld device occasionally seen today on the shelves of antique shops. It is so hopelessly old-

***Brady in the Field***
*M. B. Brady, the preeminent personality of Civil War photography, often made himself part of the image. Here, at Cold Harbor in June 1864, the straw-hatted Brady sits with Maj. Gen. Ambrose E. Burnside, who reads a copy of the* Daily Morning Chronicle, *a Washington newspaper.*

fashioned that many young people do not know what it is. But to those who lived in the late nineteenth century, the stereoscopic viewer was the equivalent of television today. It started the transformation of the American parlor from a sitting area into a home entertainment salon.

More than seventy-five years of American history was photographed in 3-D, stretching from the late 1850s to the 1930s. At the turn of the century, during one of the peaks of the long-lasting stereoscopic craze, nearly every American family room and many school rooms had a stereo viewer and a stack of stereo photographs, also called views. "The importance of this small handheld wooden device cannot be stressed enough," writes historian Alan Trachtenberg. It remade the American living room "into a microcosmic world unto itself."

Today, the stereo viewer survives in the form of the View-Master, but it is a child's toy largely devoted

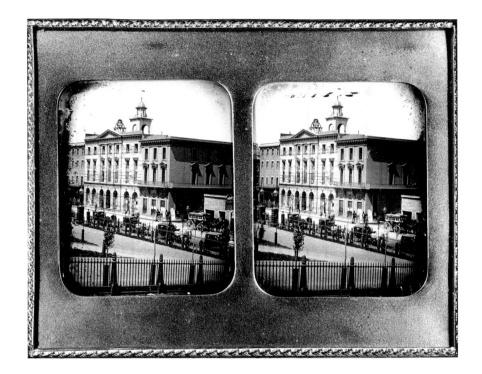

## SAN FRANCISCO CIRCA 1856

This stereo daguerreotype of San Francisco's City Hall, taken around 1856 by Robert H. Vance, came to light in 1994. It is one of first stereo photographs of an American city scene.

to cartoon and movie characters.

For nineteenth-century Americans, a stereo viewer was an intensely personal visual wonder. One disappeared under the hood of the viewer to be met instantly with a magnified photograph filled with depth, detail, and lifelike qualities. "The mind feels its way into the very depths of the picture," wrote Oliver Wendell Holmes, the nineteenth-century essayist, poet, and doctor. Holmes invented the first practical handheld viewer in 1859, two years before the Civil War started. The timing could not have been more opportune for the evolution of American photography.

When war broke out, the science of photography was only twenty-two years old. America, so full of

spirit and promise in the 1830s and 1840s, embraced photography like no other country. From 1839 to the eve of the Civil War, the craft underwent dramatic developments, just as the personal computer has so rapidly evolved in our time.

The first photographs, known as daguerreotypes, were the namesake of their inventor, the Frenchman Louis Jacques Mande Daguerre. Daguerreotypes, created on highly polished, silver-plated sheets of copper, were literally mirror images. Each daguerreotype, like a Polaroid photo, was unique. The customer received the image in a small booklike case. In the early years, the whole process had a mystical quality, and the camera was sometimes called "the dark chamber."

By 1855, the daguerreotype was on the verge of extinction. It was being eclipsed by the ambrotype, a photograph on glass. A couple of years later, the tintype, a photograph on a thin sheet of iron, rendered the ambrotype obsolete. Countless thousands of Civil War soldiers proudly posed for their ambrotype and tintype portraits, many of which survive today.

Meanwhile, in the late 1850s, yet another form of photography—the paper photograph printed from a glass-plate negative—was vigorously competing for

## A PLAY STARRING LAURA KEENE

The incredible detail of the daguerreotype reveals a playbill for *A Midsummer Night's Dream* starring actress Laura Keene, whose future held a real-life role in the Civil War. She starred in *Our American Cousin* at Ford's Theater in Washington on the night of April 14, 1865, when actor John Wilkes Booth assassinated President Abraham Lincoln.

the public's favor. The paper photograph had a tremendous advantage over the other forms of photography. A single negative could produce limitless inexpensive copies.

The paper photograph allowed photographers to

sell the portrait of a famous person as a small, single image known as a carte de visite (visiting card). In 1860, a carte de visite of Abraham Lincoln by M. B. Brady's company sold by the thousands. Lincoln said the photo helped him win the 1860 presidential election.

As the Civil War started, another new photographic phenomenon, the stereoscopic photograph, was capturing the country's imagination. A stereo view consisted of two nearly identical photographs taken with a camera with two side-by-side lenses about the same distance apart as the human eyes. When the card was viewed through a stereo viewer, the lenses enabled the eyes to combine the two photos into one, thus creating the illusion of depth.

The 3-D phenomenon was introduced to the world by Sir Charles Wheatstone of Great Britain in 1838, one year before the daguerreotype was introduced. Wheatstone coined the word "stereograph" and explained that people see objects in three dimensions because each eye sees a slightly different view.

The 3-D discoveries were soon applied to photography, and cameras were developed with side-by-side lenses. In 1849, a Scotsman, Sir David Brewster, invented the lenticular stereoscope, the first device for viewing stereo images.

Unlike the highly reflective surface of the daguerreotype, the matte finish of the paper photograph lent itself perfectly to 3-D photographs. In 1859, Edward Anthony began marketing about 175 stereo views of New York. Soon, other publishers began selling views, and with the introduction of the inexpensive, easy-to-use Holmes-Bates viewer in 1860, America's passion for stereo photographs blossomed. As the Civil War began, photographers in both the North and the South sought to make images of the great conflict, especially stereo views.

Confederate photography has often been overshadowed by the sheer output from Yankee cameras. But the Charleston, South Carolina, photographers who visited Fort Sumter and other harbor landmarks in the days after its capture took the first photos of the war.

In the North, no photographic entrepreneur was more obsessed with capturing the war on camera than M. B. Brady. When the war started, Brady had sixteen years of experience as one of the world's premier photographers. Brady and the photographers who worked for him, Alexander Gardner, Timothy O'Sullivan, and George N. Barnard among others, began chasing the army with their cameras. Although Brady himself took few, if any, of his firm's photographs, he was the driving force behind their creation and often went into the field with his operators (as the photographers were known then). "A spirit in my feet said, 'Go,' and I went," Brady told journalist George Alfred Townsend many years after the war. "I felt that I had to go."

Brady and the operators at his New York and Washington galleries were well aware that their efforts were extraordinary. Every backmark on a Brady stereo view sold during the war included the following statement:

The photographs of this series were taken directly from nature, at considerable cost. Warning is therefore given that legal proceedings will be at once instituted against any party infringing the copyright.

Brady personally went to the war's first major battle at Bull Run, where his efforts to take photos were thwarted in the Union Army rout. During the Seven Days Battle of the Peninsular Campaign of the spring of 1862, Brady operator James Gibson got close enough to the action to find a makeshift Union field hospital at Savage Station. There he took America's first great war photograph.

At Antietam Creek in western Maryland in September 1862, the Union Army of the Potomac was left in possession of a major battlefield for the first time. Alexander Gardner, Brady's Washington gallery manager, captured the first views of dead sol- diers where they fell. Gardner's series of the dead of Antietam was a stunning photographic coup that electrified New York.

In late 1862, Gardner split from Brady, who had begun to experience financial problems that would plague him the rest of his life. Gardner and Brady had become competitors by the battle of Gettysburg. Gardner arrived within days of the July 1863 battle and made another gripping series of death photos. Brady came about two weeks later, but under his personal supervision his operators captured one of the war's most famous photographs, an image of three Rebel prisoners.

In September 1863, Southern photographer George S. Cook achieved another photographic mile- stone. He took the first action photos of the Civil War from Fort Sumter while the fort was being shelled by Union gunboats. His feat was news in both the North and the South.

### THE CAMERAS

These two wet-plate cameras were manufactured and used during the Civil War. The stereographic camera (*right*) produced two side-by-side images on a four-by-ten-inch glass plate. The four-lens camera (*left*), which used a seven-by-nine-inch plate, was to facilitate the mass production of carte de visite portraits. But two of the portraits from a four-lens camera—either the top pair or the bottom pair—can also work together as a stereographic pair.

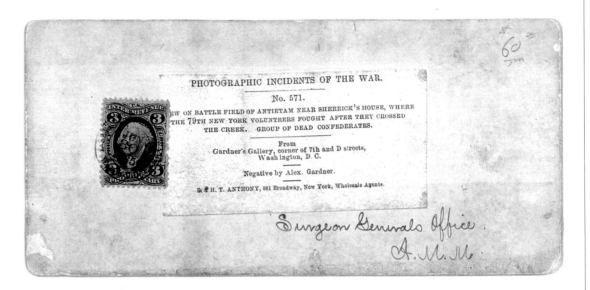

## THE BACK OF A VIEW

This original backmark from a fifty-cent Gardner Antietam stereo view (re-produced on page 44) includes a three-cent tax stamp that was canceled on June 30, 1865. A highly unpopular tax on photography was created in 1864 and repealed in late 1866.

That same month, Gardner issued a catalog of "Photographic Incidents of the War." Stereographs, priced at fifty cents each, dominated the booklet. Of the 572 photos listed for sale in Gardner's catalog, 407 were stereo views. Gardner even took mail orders, explaining that any photo could be sent safely by mail to any address.

Civil War stereo views apparently sold quite well during the war and for several years thereafter. In 1864 and 1865, Edward Anthony had a number of photographers in the field supplying him with photos. By the war's end, his catalog listed more than 1,400 stereo views. The cost was $4.50 a dozen.

By 1870, interest in war views was waning. The price had fallen to $3.50 a dozen. The financial depression of 1873 effectively killed the business. In the mid-1880s, a Hartford, Connecticut, entrepreneur named John C. Taylor obtained thousands of

the original glass plate negatives and began issuing views under his own name. By 1890, Taylor and a man named Huntington were jointly selling more than 225 different war views under the name War Photograph and Exhibition Co. Today, collectors frequently encounter Taylor and Huntington war views in excellent condition—part of a large cache of unsold views discovered in New England in the 1970s.

Taylor and Huntington views sold for thirty cents each, and the back of each Taylor and Huntington card read:

> The great value of these pictures is apparent.
> When we change the price of these war
> views, it will be to double it.

Despite this challenge, the views apparently did not sell well. And with the passing of the Taylor and

Huntington series, the three-dimensional Civil War photograph slipped into obscurity. In 1890, the first photographic history of the Civil War made on a printing press was published. *The Memorial War Book* included more than two thousand images, but all of them were reproduced as single photos. In 1911, the epic ten-volume *Photographic History of the Civil War* was published, but not a single photo was reproduced in stereo.

Oddly, stereo views were even more popular in the United States in 1911 than they were during the war. In Gettysburg, photographer W. H. Tipton's catalog listed thousands of different views of monuments and battlefield landmarks, but only a handful of actual wartime images.

Most of the books about Civil War photography published in the past forty years have continued to overlook the 3-D legacy of the war photos. Thus, in our time, the visual magnificence of Civil War stereo views has remained hidden.

Portrayed here are some of the best Civil War photos, published as they were meant to be seen, in full 3-D. One can see precisely how craggy it was on Little Round Top at Gettysburg, and how awful it was in Bloody Lane at Antietam. In bold relief, we can see the lines in Lincoln's face, and the deathly twists on the scaffold of those who conspired to murder him. We can see how blades of grass have been trampled on the battlefield and peer into the depths of a slave pen.

These wartime photographs were fresh and exciting to the nineteenth-century American, who illuminated his world with fire and still traveled by horseback.

**AN 1865 ADVERTISEMENT**

This Anthony & Co. ad for war views appeared on the back page of the May 6, 1865, edition of *Harper's Weekly*, which was devoted to coverage of Lincoln's funeral.

# A REBEL COUP AT FORT SUMTER

# CHAPTER ONE

# On April 12, 1861, years of tension between North and South exploded with the Confederate bombardment of Fort Sumter in the harbor of Charleston, South Carolina. The Civil War had begun.

After a thirty-three hour artillery duel, Union Maj. Robert Anderson agreed to surrender. He was out of ammunition and hopelessly outnumbered. The only fatality during the engagement had been a horse. In the euphoric days after the capture, at least four Charleston photographers carried their cameras to the battle-scarred fort and took the first photographs of the Civil War.

The first photographer arrived on April 15, the day after Anderson left, and made a spectacular photograph of the Confederate flag flying from a makeshift shaft. George S. Cook, a native of Connecticut, also photographed the fort. In February, Cook had come to Sumter and photographed Anderson inside the bastion. Cook's carte de visite photograph of Anderson was a top seller in New York City in the spring of 1861.

On April 17, James M. Osborn and F. E. Durbec, who operated Osborn and Durbec's Southern Stereoscopic & Photographic Depot at 223 King Street in Charleston, arrived at Fort Sumter. They produced at least twenty stereo views. Osborn and Durbec also went to Sullivan's Island and Fort Moultrie at the northern entrance to the harbor,

where they made at least thirteen additional stereo views, and exposed at least five more wet-plate stereo negatives on Morris Island to the south.

Original prints of most of Osborn and Durbec's stereo views are preserved today in the Louisiana Historical Association Collection at Tulane University in New Orleans. This is the largest known body of their work, and one of the largest collections of Confederate stereo views in existence. Other views may well exist, still to be rediscovered. If they do exist, they likely were made in the early years of the war, when chemicals, photographic paper, and other supplies were more readily available in the South.

The first opportunity to photograph the war had fallen to the Confederacy, and Southern photographers had seized it. Although their work may not have been widely seen in the North during the war, they set a standard for journalistic photography that Northern photographers would not approach for fourteen months.

*One of the First Civil War Photos*
*On April 15, 1861, the day after the Union Army surrendered Fort Sumter, a Charleston photographer took an image of the flag of the Confederate States of America flying over the fort.*

### THE PRIZE IN THE HARBOR

Fort Sumter is barely visible in the distance in this view taken by Osborn and Durbec from the site of a Dahlgren battery on Sullivan's Island a few days after the fort's capture.

### A FORMAL INSPECTION

The momentous capture gave cause for a formal inspection of the fort by top-hatted Confederate dignitaries, who stand on the parade ground between a ten-inch Columbiad gun and the shot furnace. The tall man in the center is thought to be Wade Hampton, a plantation owner who rose to the second-highest rank in the Confederate Army. The group probably also includes South Carolina Gov. Francis Pickens.

## EVIDENCE OF THE BATTLE

On the eastern parapet of Fort Sumter, with Fort Moultrie looming in the distance, several Confederate dignitaries inspect the remains of a ten-inch Columbiad damaged by its own recoil during the engagement.

## THE SPOILS OF WAR

Their confidence brimming, Confederate soldiers sit amidst debris and captured guns inside Sumter.

## A CONFEDERATE DARKROOM IN THE FIELD

This image of the Rebel gunners who fired on Fort Sumter from the Trapier Mortar Battery on Morris Island includes the portable darkroom of the photographers Osborn and Durbec, partially hidden behind the second gun. It is the only known image of a Southern photographic outfit in the field.

## MANNED FOR ACTION

Dressed in homespun outfits, the men of the Trapier Mortar Battery stand beside their guns, ready for action.

## DAMAGE AT FORT MOULTRIE

Some of the first shots of the Civil War, fired from the Union guns commanded by Capt. Abner Doubleday at Fort Sumter, blew holes in the western barracks of Fort Moultrie on Sullivan's Island.

## WHERE UNION SHELLS HIT THEIR MARK

The damage was extensive to the western barracks, which faced Fort Sumter and bore the brunt of the shells fired by the Union defenders.

# THE
# FIRST
# YEAR

# CHAPTER TWO

# Three months after Fort Sumter

was captured by the South, the Union and Confederate armies fought the first major land battle at Bull Run near Manassas in northern Virginia. Photographer M. B. Brady, eager to capture the war with his wet-plate cameras, rode out from Washington along with hundreds of other civilians and dignitaries on July 21, 1861 to see the action. When the Union Army was defeated and fled toward Washington in a panic, the spectators were caught up in the pandemonium.

"I went to the first battle of Bull Run with two wagons from Washington," Brady told journalist George Alfred Townshend in 1891 in an interview five years before his death. "We stayed all night at Centreville; we got as far as Blackburne's Ford; we made pictures and expected to be in Richmond the next day, but it was not so, and our apparatus was a good deal damaged on the way back to Washington. . . ." If Brady indeed took photos that day, none have surfaced. The setback, however, did not stop Brady and his photographers from pursuing the war. During the summer and fall of 1861, they took photographs in and around Washington. Alexander Gardner, Brady's Washington gallery manager, was just as eager to photograph the war as his boss and later claimed credit for launching the ambitious photographic expeditions from the Brady gallery in 1861 and 1862.

In late 1861, Brady or Gardner sent Timothy O'Sullivan to photograph Union operations near Beaufort, South Carolina. In March 1862, Brady pho-

tographers George Barnard and James Gibson revisited the battlefield of First Bull Run with their cameras. Gibson then followed the Union Army during its unsuccessful effort to capture Richmond in Gen. George McClellan's Peninsular Campaign. At Savage Station, one day after the battle of Gaines's Mill, Gibson found a gripping, candid scene of war at a makeshift field hospital, and with his stereoscopic camera, made the first great American war photograph. It was not a photograph of a battle or a battlefield, but it was a powerful example of photojournalism nevertheless. Photography was beginning to record the reality of war.

The challenge for the Brady & Co. photographers in the war's first eighteenth months was finding a fresh battlefield to photograph. The Union Army kept losing battles and retreating from the battlefields on which they fought. But the photographers kept pursuing the troops. And they began to realize they would have plenty of opportunities. The war, which many in the North believed would be over quickly, was becoming a long-term affair, and it was getting bloodier by the day.

*A Slave Pen*
*Alexandria, Virginia.*

## LAST VESTIGES OF A "PECULIAR INSTITUTION"

These two views of African-Americans at a Union-occupied plantation near Beaufort, South Carolina, in 1862 or 1863 are published here for the first time. They are among the very few outdoor photographs depicting American slavery. The recently freed slaves work in the field under the supervision of an overseer *(top)* and stand in front of their quarters.

### INSIDE THE SLAVE PEN

One of the most popular subjects for Washington photographers early in the war was the Price, Birch & Co. slave dealership in Alexandria, Virginia. "The establishment was essentially a prison," wrote Alexander Gardner. This view by Brady & Co. underscores that statement.

No. 380.   Engine House in which John Brown was captured. Har. Ferry. Va

### A FLASHPOINT FOR GROWING TENSIONS

This engine house in Harper's Ferry, Virginia, became forever known as "John Brown's Fort" after the radical abolitionist from Kansas and his men barricaded themselves there in October, 1859, following an aborted raid on the U.S. arsenal in an effort to start a slave insurrection. Brown was captured by Marines under the command of U.S. Army Col. Robert E. Lee and hanged for treason before year's end.

*Lowell Jail—6th Mass. Regiment in foreground.*

## FIRST BLOOD

On April 19, 1861, one week after the first shots were fired at Fort Sumter, the first blood of the Civil War was shed in Baltimore. A train carrying the soldiers of the Sixth Massachusetts Regiment, on their way to Washington to help defend the capital, was attacked by a secessionist mob of Marylanders. Four soldiers were killed and seventeen were wounded. Ten civilians were killed and many more hurt. This view shows the regiment on parade in front of the Lowell, Massachusetts, jail.

## AN OFFICER FALLS, A MARTYR IS BORN

When Col. Elmer Ellsworth of the New York Fire Zouaves, a close personal friend of President Abraham Lincoln, seized a Rebel flag flying atop the Marshall House hotel in Alexandria on May 23, 1861, he was shotgunned to death by the proprietor. While souvenir hunters carried off everything movable at the hotel, Ellsworth's body lay in state in the East Room of the White House. Ellsworth was the first officer to fall in the war. He became a Northern martyr.

## THE AMATEUR BARBER

A haircut in the field was a luxury. The conditions, and the skill of the barber, often left something to be desired.

## WRITING TO FRIENDS

At Camp Essex, about eight miles from Baltimore, Maryland, there was time to mend clothes and write to friends at home in the early months of the war. The letters being written in this view no doubt were headed to Massachusetts, since the soldiers belonged to the Boston Light Artillery, also known as Cook's Battery.

## FIRST BULL RUN

The first shots of the war's first major battle were fired by the Union Army near this stone bridge over Bull Run, Virginia on the morning of July 21, 1861. By the end of the day, the Union Army was in full retreat. The Confederates destroyed the bridge when they abandoned the area shortly before George N. Barnard took this image in March 1862.

## THE STONE CHURCH IN CENTREVILLE

Thousands of Union troops marched past this stone church in Centreville, Virginia, on their way to the front at Bull Run. When the battle was over, some of the wounded were treated inside its walls.

375.	The Siege of Yorktown, Va.
[FOR DESCRIPTION OF THIS VIEW SEE THE OTHER SIDE OF THIS CARD.]

## THE PENINSULAR CAMPAIGN BEGINS

After Bull Run, Lincoln named George B. McClellan commander of the Union Army of the Potomac, and McClellan launched an offensive on Richmond in the spring of 1862 from the peninsula east of the Confederate capital. His first move was to lay siege to Yorktown. This view shows a battery of thirteen-inch sea-coast mortars.

## CUSTER FINDS A CLASSMATE

During the battle of Fair Oaks on May 31, 1862, one of the many engagements of the Peninsular Campaign, Confederate Lt. J. B. Washington was captured by Union pickets. Later, one of Washington's West Point classmates, Lt. George Armstrong Custer, noticed the prisoner and arranged for a photograph of the battlefield reunion. Custer became a legend of American history when he perished with all his men at Little Big Horn in 1876.

Entered according to Act of Congress, in the year 1862, by Gardner & Gibson, in the Clerk's Office of the District Court of the District of Columbia.

## A FIRST IN WAR PHOTOJOURNALISM

Many of the photographs of the Peninsular Campaign were taken by James F. Gibson, one of Brady's operators. Although most of Gibson's images were the static landscapes, group shots, and portraits most commonly associated with Civil War photography, one photograph stood out for its unprecedented grittiness and spontaneity. Gibson's candid view of wounded Union soldiers at a makeshift field hospital at Savage Station depicted for the first time the human wreckage of a battle.

It is the first great American war photograph. These men, including the straw-hatted soldiers of Sixteenth New York Infantry, were wounded in the battle of Gaines's Mill on June 27. In the foreground, a surgeon works on a soldier's leg wound, while the soldier holds what appears to be a compress to his head. Behind them, the ground is covered with wounded men, most of whom are too weak or too badly hurt to notice Gibson's camera. On June 29, the Confederates launched a massive counterattack on Savage Station, and most of these men were captured.

## FUGITIVE SLAVES CROSSING THE RAPPAHANNOCK

In the war's early years, whenever the Union Army entered Virginia, it became a magnet for fugitive slaves, dubbed "contrabands," many of whom became Army servants. In this August 1862 view taken during the Second Manassas campaign by Brady operator Timothy O'Sullivan, a group of fugitive slaves ford the Rappahannock River in Virginia, carrying their belongings in an oxen cart.

# THE
# BLOODIEST
# DAY

# CHAPTER THREE

# In September 1862, the war took a stunning new direction. Confederate General Robert E. Lee routed Gen. John Pope's Union Army at the second battle of Bull Run and then invaded Maryland,

sending shock waves through the North. Gen. George McClellan was appointed to replace Pope. He went after Lee. The entire country was riveted by the daily reports and rumors about Lee's invasion.

Alexander Gardner, a native of Scotland who had emigrated to the United States in 1856, was now attached to the Union Army as a civilian photographer. He was informally known as "Captain" Gardner. It is not known whether Gardner accompanied McClellan and his army during their pursuit of Lee, or came later. On September 17, McClellan and Lee clashed outside Sharpsburg, Maryland, beside the Antietam Creek. It was the bloodiest day in American history. More than twenty-two thousand Union and Confederate soldiers were killed, wounded, or reported missing. On the morning of September 19, when Lee quietly withdrew his army back into Virginia, the Yankees were left in possession of a major Eastern theater battlefield for the first time in the war. Gardner and his assistant, James Gibson, finally had something extraordinary to photograph. The Confederate dead still lay where they fell.

Gardner had two cameras, a large-plate camera

### The Bloodiest Day
*This image shows Alexander Gardner's photographic wagon on the lower bridge, or Burnside's Bridge, at the Antietam battlefield on September 21, 1862.*

that produced seven-by-nine-inch photographs and a two-lens stereoscopic camera that produced two side-by-side images on a four-by-ten-inch negative. Later, after a print was made, the two images were cut to three-by-three-inch squares, flip-flopped, and glued side by side on a three-by-six-inch card. Gardner opted to use his stereo camera exclusively for the historic first series of soldiers lying dead on a Civil War battlefield. Over the next four days, Gardner and Gibson worked as fast as the cumbersome wet-plate process would allow. Gardner's first task was to compose the photograph. As he did this, he was thinking in three dimensions. He looked for scenes with a distinct element in the foreground, and a good, deep background. Then he spread the tall wooden legs of the camera's tripod, leveled the camera, and focused the lenses. Now it was time to prepare the plate. He coated the glass plate with a syrupy collodion mixture and then ducked into the cramped and darkened back end of his horse-drawn van, where he sensitized the plate in a solution of silver nitrate. He then put the plate in a lightproof holder, carried it to the nearby camera, and slid it behind the lenses. Inside the camera, the plate was still wet when Gardner removed the caps covering the lenses and exposed the negative to sunlight for several seconds. Whether it was three seconds or thirty seconds, or somewhere in between, depended on the light, the weather, and other factors. It was often guesswork. The plate, after being exposed, had to be returned to the wagon, developed immediately, and fixed before the collodion dried. Prints would be made later on the roof of the Washington gallery.

Gardner made as many as twenty-five negatives during his first day on the Antietam battlefield. Undoubtedly, Gibson played a key role. Since Gardner took the credit for making all the negatives that day, perhaps Gibson worked in the darkroom, sensitizing and developing plates. After four days, Gardner and Gibson had about sixty photographs of the battlefield of Antietam, including twenty stereo views showing dead soldiers.

When Gardner's photographs went on display in Brady's New York gallery in an exhibition entitled *The Dead of Antietam*, the pictures stunned the city. These photographs were unlike anything anyone had ever seen. "Let him who wishes to know what war is look at this series of illustrations," wrote Dr. Oliver Wendell Holmes. "Mr. Brady has done something to bring home to us the terrible reality and earnestness of the war," the *New York Times* reported on October 20. "You will see hushed, reverent groups standing around these weird copies of

carnage, bending down to look in the pale faces of the dead, chained by the strange spell that dwells in dead men's eyes."

The photographs were all the more startling in 3-D, and all, of course, were for sale. Stereographs were fifty cents each. Album cards and cartes de visite, with half of a stereo view presented as a single, two-dimensional photo, were twenty-five cents each. The stereo views outsold the album cards and cartes de visite.

Copies of photos were rushed to *Harper's Weekly*, the *Life* magazine of its day, whose artists made hand-drawn renditions because photoreproduction in newspapers was not possible then. Nine Antietam photos were reproduced as woodcut engravings in the center-spread picture page of the October 18, 1862 edition.

"The living that throng Broadway care little perhaps for the Dead of Antietam, but we fancy they would jostle less carelessly down the great thoroughfare, saunter less at their ease, were a few dripping bodies, fresh from the field, laid along the pavement," the *Times* reported. "If [Brady] has not brought bodies and laid them in our door-yards and along streets, he has done something very like it."

There is no record of Brady's reaction to his exhibition of Antietam photos, or of Gardner's reaction, but we know that their success at Antietam served only to stimulate their obsession with capturing the war on camera.

Entered according to the Act of Congress, in the year 1862, by ALEX. GARDNER, in the Clerk's Office of the District Court of the District of Columbia.

## ANTIETAM CREEK

This three-arch stone toll bridge carried traffic on the Sharpsburg and Boonsboro Turnpike across Antietam Creek. It was known as the middle bridge. Little action took place here, but Gardner made at least eleven photographs of the span.

552.    Dunker Church, Antietam, Sept. 17, 1862.
[FOR DESCRIPTION OF THIS VIEW SEE THE OTHER SIDE OF THIS CARD.]

## THE DUNKER CHURCH

At the center of the human slaughter at Antietam sat the simple, whitewashed church of the Dunkers, a pacifistic sect whose members refused to bear arms. The war found them anyway. During and after the battle, their shell-damaged church was a shelter for wounded on both sides. In the foreground are the bodies of dead Confederates.

Entered according to act of Congress, in the year 1862, by Alexander Gardner, in the Clerk's Office of the District Court of the District of Columbia.

## THEY LAY AS THEY FELL

This damaged Brady view, one of the most famous Antietam photographs, shows dead Confederates, probably of Gen. William E. Starke's Louisiana brigade, lying as they fell at the fence along Hagerstown Pike during the furious fighting in and around the cornfield.

## TOURING THE FIELD OF THE DEAD

The soldiers here are Louisiana boys, frozen in rigor mortis and swelling after two days in the September heat. But the grotesque sights did not stop sight-seers, as evidenced by the civilian buggy in the background on the far side of Hagerstown Pike.

Entered acc... GATHERED TOGETHER FOR BURIAL AFTER THE BATTLE OF ANTIETAM.

## GATHERED TOGETHER FOR BURIAL

While Gardner worked quickly to record as many battlefield scenes as he could, burial crews gathered the dead for mass burial in shallow graves. Pictured here are at least twenty-five of the estimated twenty-seven hundred Confederate soldiers killed in action at Antietam.

Entered according to Act of Congress, in the year 1862, by Alex. Gardner, in the Clerk's Office of the District Court of the District of Columbia.

## THE PRIVILEGES OF THE VICTOR

In war, the winners bury their own dead first. At Antietam, two days after the battle, Gardner found the grave of Lt. John A. Clark of the Seventh Michigan Infantry next to the body of an unburied Confederate. In the background is a fence dismantled during the battle by advancing soldiers.

Although photographs were widely marketed during the war, it was not possible to reproduce them directly in the mass media because the halftone photoengraving process had not yet been invented. Many Civil War photographs, however, were reproduced as woodcut engravings in *Harper's Weekly*. This image was one of nine published as woodcuts in the October 18, 1862, edition.

HARPER'S WEEKLY.

## THE SUNKEN ROAD . . .

When two Union divisions veered off their original course, they found two brigades of Confederates waiting for them in a sunken farm road. The battle for this road inflicted heavy losses on both sides. Here, burial parties are at work at a section of the road that had been occupied by the Second North Carolina Regiment.

## . . . BECAME "BLOODY LANE."

The stories the soldiers told about the packed bodies in the sunken road were no exaggeration. These men also were probably from North Carolina.

## THE DAMAGE DONE BY A SHELL

Until this photograph is seen in three dimensions, one does not readily perceive the extent of damage inflicted on the body of the fallen young Confederate at left. Undoubtedly struck by a shell, he fell on the southern section of the battlefield not far from Burnside's Bridge.

## LINCOLN VISITS THE BATTLEFIELD

On October 3 and 4, 1862, two and a half weeks after the battle, President Lincoln visited Antietam to find out why McClellan was not pursuing Lee.

Alexander Gardner returned to Antietam and made several images of Lincoln's visit, including this stereo view of a group at Union Army headquarters. McClellan stands fourth from the right. The seated man at left is Ward Hill Lamon, Lincoln's bodyguard and former law partner.

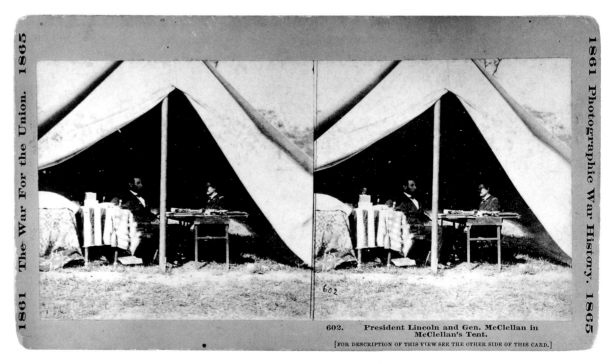

602. President Lincoln and Gen. McClellan in McClellan's Tent.

[FOR DESCRIPTION OF THIS VIEW SEE THE OTHER SIDE OF THIS CARD.]

## A TENSE MEETING

Lincoln and McClellan had a strained relationship, and the tension between them seems to be reflected in this view of them in McClellan's tent. A captured Confederate battle flag sits on the ground at left. One month and three days after this photograph was taken, the president relieved McClellan of his command.

# ABRAHAM LINCOLN: A MAN FOR THE AGES

# CHAPTER FOUR

# There are 130 different photographs of Abraham Lincoln. Of these, only nine are known to have been sold as stereo views.

But for almost a hundred years after his death, there was a secret about many photographs of Lincoln that almost no one knew. At least twenty-five more Lincoln photographs were made with three-lens or four-lens cameras, which meant that all of those images of the most recognizable face in American history could, potentially, be viewed in 3-D.

During a lifetime of collecting, Dayton, Ohio, artist Lloyd Ostendorf has painstakingly reconstructed, image by image, nearly all of those twenty-five Lincoln photographs so that they can be viewed in 3-D. Ostendorf became obsessed with Lincoln's face at the age of twelve. In 1938, when he was twenty-one, he began collecting Lincoln photographs.

Ostendorf did not learn until the 1950s that many Lincoln photos were taken with a multiple-lens camera. Once he discovered this, Ostendorf set about trying to find the images from each lens of every multiple-lens photo. He pored over the hundreds of Lincoln carte de visite photos already in his collection and learned how to recognize the minute differences in seemingly identical photographs that proved they were from different lenses. He discovered new multiple-lens images. And for any two images that he suspected came from side-by-side lenses, he performed the conclu-

sive test—an examination with a stereo viewer. Ostendorf set the two images next to each other, about an inch apart, and he viewed them as one through the viewer. If Lincoln appeared in 3-D, Ostendorf knew that the images were not identical and came from side-by-side lenses.

Today, almost sixty years later, Ostendorf is one of the world's foremost authorities on Lincoln photographs. He coauthored *Lincoln in Photographs*, the only book of every known pose. He has personally discovered, first published, or identified twenty-four previously unknown photographs of Lincoln and owns one of the finest collections of Lincoln images in existence anywhere, including hundreds of Lincoln cartes de visite, dozens of other images, and a half-dozen original glass-plate negatives.

Ostendorf, who is now in his seventies, has never lost his enthusiasm for Lincoln photographs. He continues to search for—and to find—undiscovered Lincoln photographs, and to debunk photos spuriously passed off as Lincoln. What follows are some of the best Lincoln photographs in 3-D from the Ostendorf collection.

***The Broken Plate***
*Lincoln's unforgettable face, captured on April 10, 1864, is framed by the jagged edges of a broken glass plate negative in the Ostendorf collection.*

## OSTENDORF'S GREATEST STEREOSCOPIC FIND

Lloyd Ostendorf's collection includes the rarest of the rare—a handful of the actual glass-plate negatives of Abraham Lincoln. In 1955, he paid several hundred dollars to the aged son of a Civil War veteran for an old album of rare photos as well as the upper right-hand negative from a four-lens image of Lincoln. Nineteen years later, Ostendorf discovered and purchased for a thousand dollars the upper left-hand negative from the same sitting. The photo was made by the photographer Lewis E. Walker in 1863.

## THE 1861 INAUGURATION

The dome of the U.S. Capitol was still unfinished when Abraham Lincoln took his first oath of office on March 4, 1861. In the distance, Brig. Gen. Montgomery C. Meigs, an amateur photographer, aimed a stereoscopic camera at the ceremony and took the upper image. In the lower photo, an unknown photographer recorded Lincoln's inaugural parade as it moved down Pennsylvania Avenue. This photograph is published here for the first time.

## THE SWOLLEN HAND

After shaking the hands of thousands of
well-wishers, president-elect Lincoln had a
swollen right hand when he sat for this
photograph by Alexander Gardner in
Brady's Washington gallery, probably on
February 24, 1861. He kept his hand closed
or hidden during this photograph session,
his first in Washington. Reproduced here
are the right- and left-hand images from a
three-lens camera.

## THE PRESIDENT STANDS
## FOR A PICTURE

One of M. B. Brady's operators, the Frenchman
Thomas Le Mere, prevailed upon Lincoln to
pose for a full-length standing shot at Brady's
gallery on or about April 17, 1863. Le Mere
used a camera with three horizontal lenses.
Reproduced here are the first and second
images, discovered and identified by Ostendorf.

## LINCOLN IN PROFILE

The famous Lincoln profile was captured on February 9, 1864, by Anthony Berger, who succeeded Gardner as manager of Brady's Washington gallery. It was one of seven poses in that sitting. A close variant of this pose was used to design the Lincoln penny. These two images are from the lower left and right lenses on the four-lens camera Berger used.

## FATHER AND SON

Lincoln and his son, Tad, study a Brady album at the photographer's Washington gallery on February 9, 1864. The photo was taken with a multiple-lens camera by Berger and is one of the most popular of all Lincoln images. Ostendorf was the first to find the different images and reassemble them as a stereo pair. The left image is vignetted.

## THE COMMANDER-IN-CHIEF

This regal portrait was taken by M.B. Brady with a four-lens camera in Washington on January 8, 1864. The lower left and right images are reproduced here.

52

## THE SECOND INAUGURATION

This slightly out-of-focus photograph by Alexander Gardner of the second inauguration of Abraham Lincoln on March 4, 1865, is the only known stereo view of the occasion. Lincoln is the first person seated to the left of the lectern. The image was unknown to Lincoln scholars until identified by Ostendorf in the mid-1980s.

Entered according to Act of Congress in the year 1865, by E & H T Anthony & Co, in clerk's office of District Court of U,S, for the So, District of New York,

## A FUZZY-HAIRED LINCOLN

This photograph was taken with a four-lens camera in early 1865, when Lincoln had close-cropped hair. The bottom pair of images was issued as a stereo view in 1865 by the E. & H. T. Anthony Company, which also marketed the photo as a carte de visite.

ABRAHAM LINCOLN, Pres't U. S.

ABRAHAM LINCOLN, Pres't U. S.

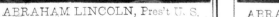

Entered according to Act of Congress, by Alex. Gardner, in the year 1865, in the Clerk's Office of the District Court for the District of Columbia

## THE LAST FORMAL SITTING

The war has taken its toll on the president in this multiple-lens portrait from his last formal sitting on February 5, 1865, at Gardner's gallery in Washington. Gardner's camera captured a haggard, time-worn president who had just ten weeks to live.

**THE HOME HE NEVER RETURNED TO**

After Lincoln was assassinated in 1865, his home in Springfield, Illinois, was draped in mourning cloth. Here his horse is posed in front of the house.

# GETTYSBURG

# CHAPTER FIVE

# The greatest battle of the Civil War was fought outside the little town of Gettysburg, Pennsylvania, on July 1, 2, and 3, 1863.

It ended Lee's second invasion of the North and was the beginning of the long, slow death of the Confederacy. More than fifty-one thousand men were killed, wounded, or reported missing, and several dozen of the mangled and lifeless bodies of Gettysburg casualties were immortalized by Alexander Gardner's camera before they were laid to rest in makeshift battlefield graves.

Gardner had opened his own gallery in Washington after splitting from Brady in late 1862 or early 1863. Whether it was the lack of professional recognition working in Brady's shadow, Brady's financial problems, a desire to be in charge of his own destiny, or a combination of all these things, Gardner resigned. He became Brady's chief competitor.

Gardner, along with James Gibson and Timothy O'Sullivan, were the first photographers at the battlefield, arriving two days after the final day's battle. Soldiers from both sides were still lying where they fell. Gardner's gallery marketed fifty-two different Gettysburg stereo views, more than thirty of which depicted the human carnage.

Brady arrived around July 15, some ten days after Gardner. By then, all the bodies had been buried. But Brady saw Gettysburg with an distinctively different eye. Gardner's photographs are gritty journalistic images, and convey a feeling that they were

**The Dead Sharpshooter**
*This same dead Confederate soldier appears in the image at the bottom of page 60.*

taken in the haste of making as many as possible.

Brady had a more artistic vision. The images his operators took provided more of a sense of place. He filled gaps that Gardner missed, capturing landscapes and panoramas of Gettysburg, as well as portraits of old John Burns, the battle's civilian hero. On Seminary Ridge, he came upon three Rebel prisoners, and one of his cameramen made one of the Civil War's most renowned photographs. Most of Brady's photos were stereo views, and they were largely marketed through the E. and H. T. Anthony Company.

Other photographers visited Gettysburg, too, but the work of Gardner and Brady stood out. Interestingly, both men continued to receive generally equal credit for their Civil War photographic accomplishments for more than fifty years after the war. In the twentieth century, however, Brady's name began to overwhelm his rival's, particularly with the publication of two biographies that gave him credit for Gardner's work. Photohistorian William A. Frassanito has done much to restore Gardner to his proper place, beginning with the publication of the landmark *Gettysburg: A Journey in Time* in 1975.

274.          The Horrors of War.
[FOR DESCRIPTION OF THIS VIEW SEE THE OTHER SIDE OF THIS CARD.]

## THE HORROR OF WAR

Perhaps the most graphic of all Civil War photos, this Alexander Gardner image was taken on July 5, 1863, three days after this Confederate fell.

Gardner planted the rifle and the artillery shell. He entitled the view: "War, effect of a shell on a Confederate soldier." William A. Frassanito, however, has found strong evidence to suggest the body had been mutilated by wild pigs.

Entered according to Act of Congress, in the year 1863, by Alex. Gardner, in the Clerk's Office of the District Court of the District of Columbia.

### MEADE'S HEADQUARTERS

The Union commander, Maj. Gen. George G. Meade, made his headquarters in a home behind Cemetery Ridge owned by a widow, Mrs. Lydia A. Leister. The damage shown in this Gardner photograph was caused by the tremendous two-hour Confederate cannonade that preceded Pickett's Charge. The barrage forced Meade to seek new quarters.

Entered according to Act of Congress, in the year 1863, by Alex. Gardner, in the Clerk's Office of the District Court of the District of Columbia.

### GARDNER'S DARKROOM WAGON

Behind these fallen Confederates, probably South Carolinians or Georgians who fell near the Rose Farm, sits Gardner's darkroom wagon. The horses undoubtedly were unhitched to graze while Gardner made photographs of these and other nearby bodies from several angles.

## UNFIT FOR SERVICE

Gardner's caption for this July 6, 1863, photo of a wrecked artillery limber was "Unfit for Service—On the battlefield of Gettysburg." This was one of more than fifteen hundred horses killed in the battle.

Entered according to Act of Congress, in the year 1863, by Alex. Gardner, in the Clerk's Office of the District Court of the District of Columbia.

## THE DEAD SHARPSHOOTER

In the best-known example of photographic manipulation during the Civil War, Gardner made this and several similar photographs of a dead Southerner in Devil's Den, then dragged the body some forty yards to a Confederate sharpshooter's position and photographed the famous "Home of a Rebel Sharpshooter." The soldier was probably not a sharpshooter, but a regular infantryman.

253.     The Slaughter Pen at Gettysburg.
[FOR DESCRIPTION OF THIS VIEW SEE THE OTHER SIDE OF THIS CARD.]

## THE SLAUGHTER PEN

The "Slaughter Pen" at Gettysburg, so named by Gardner, was at the foot of the Round Tops. These four Confederates were probably killed during the second day's fighting. The fact that Gardner, in composing the scene, purposely included the trees and rocks in the foreground suggests he was well aware of how dramatic they would look in 3-D.

Entered according to Act of Congress in the year 1862, by Alex. Gardner, in the Clerk's Office of the District Court of the District of Columbia.

## "ALL OVER NOW"

Gardner's succinct caption underscored the finality of this signature Gettysburg image. He made the photograph along Plum Run near the so-called Slaughter Pen on July 6 or 7, 1863. This Confederate had died during the assault of July 2.

## CULP'S HILL

Two of M. B. Brady's assistants posed behind a line of stone and log breastworks on the eastern slope of Culp's Hill, gazing toward the Confederate position. New York troops built these fortifications on the morning of the second day's battle. That evening, just before sunset, the Confederates launched an unsuccessful assault against them.

## A BATTLEFIELD PANORAMA

In this sweeping Brady view, the heart of the Union defensive position on Little Round Top, crucial in the second day's battle, dominates the foreground. In the distance is Cemetery Hill and, to the left of the grove of trees, the fateful area where Pickett's charge ground to a bloody halt on the epic third day of the battle.

## THE LUTHERAN THEOLOGICAL SEMINARY

This classic Brady photograph shows the Lutheran Theological Seminary, built in 1832.

During the battle, it was used by the Union army, then the Confederates, then the Union again as an observatory and hospital. It was still being used as a hospital when this view was taken around July 15.

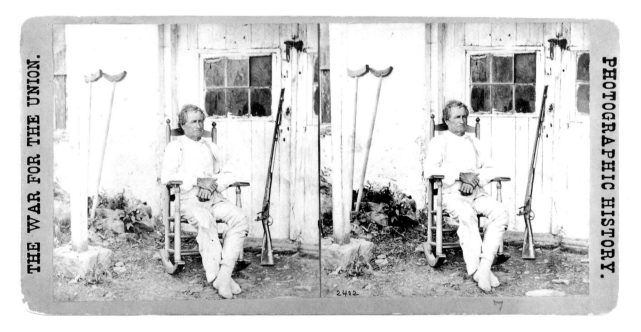

## A HOMETOWN HERO

John L. Burns, 69, a veteran of the War of 1812 and a staunch patriot, shouldered his flintlock musket and marched to the Union battle lines on the first day of the battle. He was wounded three

times and became a national hero. Even Lincoln requested an audience when he came to Gettysburg to dedicate the cemetery. Burns's story had become known by the time Brady reached Gettysburg around July 15, 1863, and he made several images of Burns with his musket and crutches.

# A SENSE
# OF ACTION

# CHAPTER SIX

# Nothing is more misunderstood

about the photographic history of the Civil War than action photography. Did any photographer actually capture images in the midst of combat? Older histories misidentified certain photos, often purposely, as having been taken under fire. Some recent photo histories categorically state that there are no combat photos, asserting that exposure times were too long to capture action.

In fact, there *are* Civil War action photos. Three Confederate photographs taken in Fort Sumter during an intense Union bombardment on September 8, 1863—reproduced together here for the first time—establish that Southern photographer George S. Cook and his assistant, J. M. Osborne, were the world's first combat photographers. Their accomplishment is little known today. But it was documented in both Northern and Southern newspapers during the war, as well as in the 1890 history *The Defense of Charleston Harbor*.

As for Northern combat photography, a less-compelling argument can be made for a photograph purportedly showing the smoke from an exploded Rebel shell at Dutch Gap Canal in Virginia in 1864. Still, it is an intriguing image. And there are other candid Civil War photos that were not taken under fire but exude an uncommon sense of spontaneity and action.

Cook's photos were so extraordinary, they made

*A Bleak Existence inside Fort Sumter*
*This 1864 image by George S. Cook showed the destruction caused by frequent Union shelling of Fort Sumter, and one of the Rebels who grimly defended it.*

headlines. "The *Ironsides* and Two Monitors Taken—A Bold Feat" the *Charleston Daily Courier* reported on September 12, four days after Cook made the images. The headline used "taken" as a pun; the vessels were not physically captured, but photographed "amid the smoke of battle in which they were wreathed." It was "one of the most remarkable acts ever recorded in the history of war," the paper reported, adding, "The feat itself is unparalleled, as far as we know...."

In the North, the *Providence (Rhode Island) Daily Journal* reported the story on October 20, 1863, under the headline "Photographing Fort Sumter Under Difficulties." The story was reprinted from the *Mobile (Alabama) Advertiser*, which had received the report from its Charleston correspondent.

"Shot and shell were flying in profusion, but, nevertheless, arranging their chemicals in one of the dark crevices of the fort, and making use of a broken carriage in place of the customary tripod, the work was begun," the story said. "Subsequently, an admirable battle scene was taken, representing the *Ironsides* and two monitors, wreathed in their own smoke, while delivering their fire on Fort Moultrie."

It has been assumed that Cook took only one photograph of the Union gunboats in action. But on June 29, 1996, while studying reproductions of the image in several books, I discovered that Cook had actually made two photographs from the parapet. The differences in the two images are minute but clearly perceptible. Even more remarkably, Cook created the two photographs to be used together as a stereo view. When they are mounted side by side and viewed through a stereo viewer, Cook's combat scene comes alive in 3-D. That was Cook's aim. The Charleston correspondent of the *Mobile Advertiser* reported: "I learn that it is intended, after a time, to make these pictures public, and to reduce them to stereoscopic dimensions."

After finishing his work on photographing the parapet, Cook set up his camera inside the fort and took a series of images. In one, he captured the smoke from an exploding shell fired by the Union gunboat *Weehawken*. Original prints of this photo have been retouched, causing some historians to doubt its authenticity. But the tremendous Union bombardment of Sumter and Moultrie on September 8 is well documented, as is the fact that Cook was there with his camera.

COOK'S "EXPLODING SHELL" PHOTOGRAPH

## THE FIRST COMBAT PHOTOGRAPH IN THREE DIMENSIONS

Charleston photographer George S. Cook came to Fort Sumter on September 8, 1863, because the Confederates wanted a photographic record of the destruction wrought by weeks of intense Union bombardment. That same day, the Union monitor *Weehawken* was stuck on a sandbar and exposed to Confederate guns at Fort Moultrie. To protect the *Weehawken*, the Union fleet began shelling Fort Moultrie at about 11 a.m. The battle lasted five hours and was "probably the severest naval engagement in American history up to that time," wrote former CSA Major John Johnson in *The Defense of Charleston Harbor*.

Cook took his camera to Sumter's parapet to photograph the attacking ships. He had to keep low, which explains why the immediate foreground fills the bottom of the image. The lead gunboat, the *New Ironsides*, belching smoke from its twenty heavy guns, was then the most powerful battleship in the world. Cook had only a single-lens camera, so he improvised to make a stereo view. He exposed one photograph, moved the camera slightly to the right to attain stereo-

scopic separation, then took the second photograph. By this time, the ships were further up the harbor. Thus, many viewers will see two sets of ships in this view. But the foreground should still be in vivid 3-D.

Although aground, the *Weehawken* fought furiously. Fort Sumter's guns had been silenced by the Union fleet on September 1, but the Rebels still occupied it. Some movement in the fort—perhaps Cook at work—drew the *Weehawken's* attention. It began firing and sent forty-six shells into Fort Sumter that day. Cook was not deterred.

"Mr. Cook requested permission to go outside the fort and take a picture of the exterior from the water, but it was thought that this would draw additional fire from the fleet, and the project was abandoned," the *Charleston Daily Courier* reported.

Cook's achievement was long remembered by his contemporaries. Photographer Timothy O'Sullivan, writing of his wartime adventures in 1869, remembered an unnamed "courageous operator" at Fort Sumter in 1863. Others took cover, O'Sullivan wrote, "but the photographer stuck to his work, and the pictures made on that memorable occasion are among the most interesting of the war."

## THE CASE FOR NORTHERN COMBAT PHOTOGRAPHY

The caption on the back of this obscure and unpublished Civil War photograph of Dutch Gap Canal in December 1864 reads: "The mist arising against the bank is caused by a rebel shell, which exploded just as this view was being photographed."

If they were indeed under fire, the soldiers in this picture appear unruffled. The soldier at right, however, turned his head during the exposure. In another, nearly identical photo, his head is perfectly still. There is plenty of written documentation that the workers at Dutch Gap Canal, a Union engineering boondoggle during the siege of Petersburg, were frequently harassed by Confederate mortars. They may have been used to the shelling.

The photograph becomes more intriguing when compared with an 1882 drawing and written account in "Anthony's Photographic Bulletin" of a photographer under fire at Dutch Gap during the Civil War. The drawing shows a cameraman with his camera, under fire at approximately the same location where the Dutch Gap "action" photo was taken.

In the written account, Civil War photographer A. J. Russell states that the Confederates were firing shells every few minutes, but the photographer, who may have been T. C. Roche, intended to take a final photograph from the "most exposed" position. "He was within a few rods of the place when down came with the roar of a whirlwind a ten-inch shell, which exploded, throwing the dirt in all directions; but nothing daunted and shaking the dust from his head and camera he quickly moved to the spot, and placing it over the pit made by the explosion, exposed his plate as coolly as if there was no danger. . . ," Russell wrote. "I asked him if he was scared. 'Scared?' he said. 'Two shots never fell in the same place.'"

It is not known precisely who took this Dutch Gap image. The account does not precisely jibe with the photograph. Civil War photohistorians question the accuracy of the caption. But given the quirks of Civil War photography, it is possible that there is a correlation between the image and the reminiscence.

Prof. Lowe observing the battle of Fair Oaks, from his balloon.

## PROFESSOR LOWE OBSERVING THE BATTLE OF FAIR OAKS

While Civil War photographers were generally unable to capture battle scenes, they did take images that conveyed a sense of battle. In this view from the Peninsular Campaign in 1862, Professor Thaddeus Lowe was said to be watching the battle of Fair Oaks from his balloon.

Entered according to Act of Congress, in the year 1862, by Alex. Gardner, in the Clerk's Office of the District Court of the District of Columbia.

## THE SMOKE FROM ANTIETAM CAMPFIRES

This photograph from the Antietam battlefield by Alexander Gardner was said to have been taken on September 17, 1862, the day of the battle. Although Gardner never specifically claimed it to be a combat photo, others have for more than one hundred years, even in recently published books. But in 1963, it was determined that the camera location was at McClellan's headquarters about a mile east of the battlefield. Although the man in the foreground has his binoculars trained on the battlefield, the rising smoke is from campfires.

## IN THE MIDST OF A HASTY RETREAT

During a hasty retreat of the Army of the Potomac from Culpeper, Virginia, in early October, 1863, photographer A. J. Russell took several remark-able views of the withdrawal to Manassas. From atop a boxcar on a soon-to-depart train (*above*) Russell photographed part of the village. The unpublished image below is identified on the original view as the last train from Culpeper, hurriedly packed with supplies and furniture.

## RARE VIEWS OF A BURNING BUILDING

Published here for the first time *(above)* is an exceedingly rare, perhaps unique, Civil War scene of a blazing fire as it consumes a building. In another view *(below)*, the top of the burning build-ing is barely visible behind the train car as a group of Union soldiers observes the fire. The original captions on these views said former slaves, known as "contrabands," had set their quarters on fire and were "skedaddling" with the fleeing army.

### LOOKOUT VALLEY, TENNESSEE

Although the far-off smoke is probably from brush-clearing operations, it is easy to imagine that this is what a photograph of distant combat would have looked like if Civil War photographers had managed to make one.

### WATCHING THE BATTLE OF NASHVILLE

Somewhere in the hidden distance, the battle of Nashville rages on December 15, 1864, as the Confederate initiative under Gen. John Bell Hood to retake Nashville is routed by the attacks of Union Gen. George Thomas.

762.    Destruction of a Railroad Bridge.
[FOR DESCRIPTION OF THIS VIEW SEE THE OTHER SIDE OF THIS CARD.]

## DESTRUCTION OF A RAILROAD BRIDGE

It was rare during the Civil War for a photographer to capture even the smoldering aftermath of the war's destruction. But photographer

Timothy O'Sullivan succeeded on May 26, 1864, with his image of the still-smoking wreckage of a railroad bridge over the North Anna River in Virginia. The bridge was destroyed by the Confederates to slow the Union advance.

## SHERMAN'S MEN TEAR UP ATLANTA

Some of the war's most spontaneous images were made by George A. Barnard when Sherman occu-

pied Atlanta in 1864. As smoke from their fires drifts across the landscape, Sherman's boys tear up the railroad in downtown Atlanta before setting fire to much of the city.

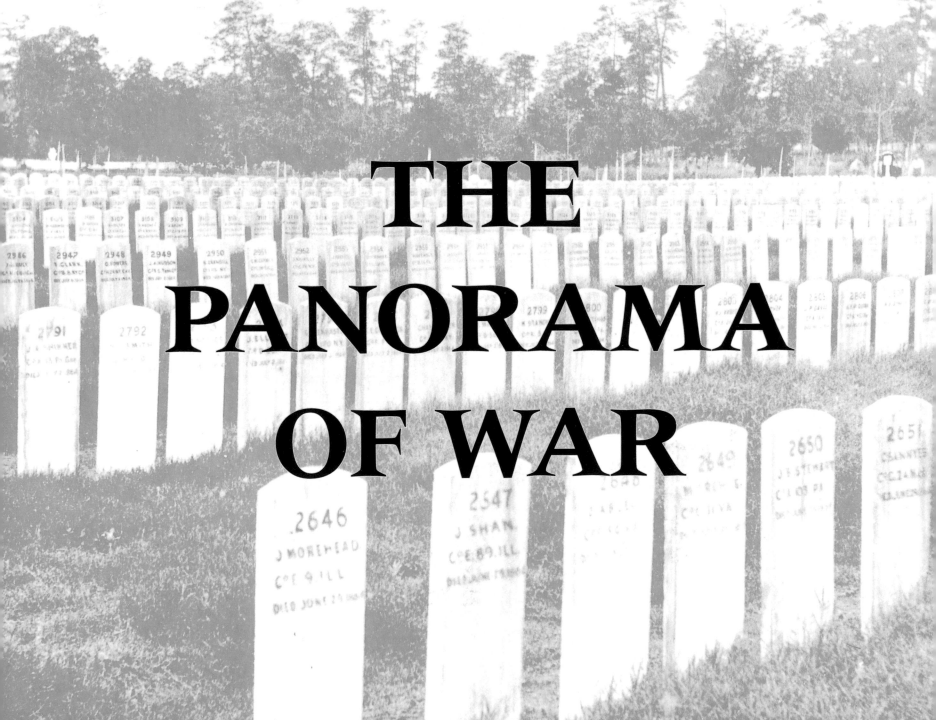

# CHAPTER SEVEN

# Month after month, year after year, the war dragged on. For the soldiers, one of the most common expressions in letters home was how awful the war was, and how they hoped it would end soon.

There was little of the glory one sees in modern battle lithographs. The war was sweat, mud, sickness and hardship interspersed with moments of sheer bloody terror, followed by pain, suffering, sadness, and, occasionally, the exhausted euphoria of victory.

Over the course of four years of civil war, photographers managed to capture images that give us an unvarnished view of the conflict. Someone had to bring the dead in from the battlefield and bury them. Someone had to amputate the mangled limbs of the wounded. Something had to be done with the prisoners, and many hundreds of captured Confederates were shipped deep into the North to a prison at Elmira, New York, where a local photographer in the business of selling Home Views made pictures of their bleak environment.

There is no romance in these photographs. This was the real war. The significance of the work of the camera in the theaters of conflict was recognized in the journals of the day. "Brady's album photographs of the war, and its persons and places, are the portraits of the living time," the *Harper's New Monthly Magazine* reported in November 1862.

***The Graveyard at Andersonville***
*Some thirteen thousand federal prisoners died at the notorious Confederate prison at Andersonville, Georgia, sometimes at a rate of more than five an hour.*

"There is nothing here that is not in nature. The interest of these vivid pictures is very great. A set of them—there are more than five hundred—gives you a picture of the whole theater of war in Virginia. In these days of Photographic albums, what is so stirring, so touching, as these views!"

As the war progressed, the Northern photographers became ever more prolific and creative. But in the blockaded South, chemicals, glass plates, and other supplies became scarce or unavailable, and photography dried up. The indefatigable George S. Cook, however, succeeded in making photographs, with some interruptions, from the beginning until the end of the war. Initially, he had chemicals shipped to him labeled as "quinine." When the Union blockade tightened, Cook purchased stock in several blockade-running ships, and not only made profits from them, but used them to obtain his supplies. By 1863, however, his fees had doubled—ranging from four to twenty-five dollars. And he did not accept Confederate currency. He required payment in gold.

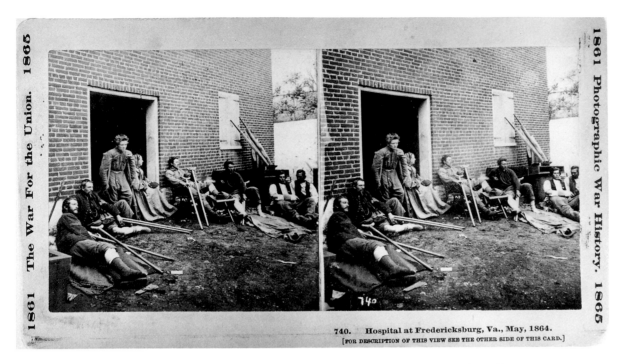

740.    Hospital at Fredericksburg, Va., May, 1864.

[FOR DESCRIPTION OF THIS VIEW SEE THE OTHER SIDE OF THIS CARD.]

## WOUNDED AT FREDERICKSBURG

In this classic war image taken by Gardner's brother, James, on May 20, 1864, Union soldiers of the Sixth Corps wounded at the Wilderness or Spotsylvania are shown recovering at a Sanitary Commission hospital behind a Charles Street warehouse in Fredericksburg.

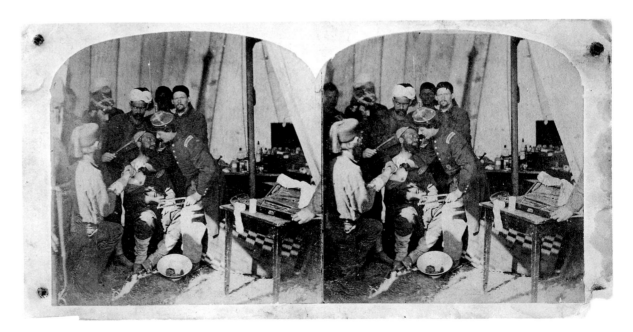

## AN AMPUTATION

Although staged, this 1861 scene of a Fifth New York Zouave about to have his arm amputated was all too real for many thousands of soldiers in the Civil War. The doctor at left is Surgeon Rufus Gilbert. At right, holding the saw, is Asst. Surgeon B. Ellis Martin.

## THE EMBALMER

Those who could afford it sometimes had the luxury of having their fallen loved ones embalmed in the field before being returned home for burial. This is Dr. Richard Burr, embalming surgeon of the Army of the James. Embalmers promised work that was "free of infection and odor."

1861  The War For the Union.  1865

1861  Photographic War History.  1865

918.    Collecting Remains of the Dead.
[FOR DESCRIPTION OF THIS VIEW SEE THE OTHER SIDE OF THIS CARD.]

## REMAINS FROM A PAST ENGAGEMENT

In the early summer of 1865, after the war ended, burial parties moved across old battlefields in Virginia to recover the bodies of hastily buried Union soldiers. These dead likely fell at Cold Harbor in June 1864.

**ON THE DECK OF THE MONITOR**

In July 1862, four months after its fight with the

*Merrimac*, or *Virginia*, the Union ironclad *Monitor* was photographed by James F. Gibson, with battle damage still evident on its turret.

THE WAR FOR THE UNION.

PHOTOGRAPHIC HISTORY.

**A DOUBLE-TURRETED IRONCLAD**

The success of the *Monitor* led to the construction

of even bigger low-draft ironclads for the Union Navy, included the double-turreted *Onandaga*, shown here in the James River in Virginia.

## LIBBY PRISON, RICHMOND

The old Libby & Son warehouse on the Richmond waterfront was the South's most notorious prison, if only because so many literate Northern officers were imprisoned there and wrote of their experiences. After the war, Libby Prison was the most photographed building in Richmond.

## REBEL PRISON, ELMIRA, NEW YORK

Conditions were not exactly ideal for Confederate POWs in Northern confinement. This remarkable photograph by Elmira photographer J. E. Larkin shows an evening roll call at the prison in 1865, with sergeants in front of the prisoners, calling each captive by name. At the end of the war, the Elmira tally was 2,917 deaths, 17 escapes, and 8,970 parolees.

## TWO NEW PHOTOGRAPHS OF GRANT'S VICKSBURG CAMPAIGN

These two photographs from the Vicksburg campaign in 1863 are published here for the first time. They were made by the Cincinnati photographers Barr and Young, who followed Ohio units to the front. Above, a riverboat steams past a disabled gun at Davis Bend near Vicksburg. Below, riverboats and a hospital ship are crowded into Chickasaw Bayou a few miles north of the city.

### FOUR OHIO DRUMMER BOYS

This camp photograph of the four drummer boys of Company B, 102nd Ohio Volunteers, is also published here for the first time. From left to right are J. W. Bingham, H. A. Bailey, Walter Hill, and Frank Brown. Bailey sent the view to his family in Wooster, Ohio, in a letter mailed from Vicksburg.

GRANT
TAKES
OVER

# CHAPTER EIGHT

# During the second week of March

1864, President Abraham Lincoln appointed Gen. Ulysses S. Grant, who had captured Vicksburg, to command the Union armies. Grant left the western theater and came east to do battle with Lee. Grant was a fighter, and the two armies clashed in bitter battles in the Wilderness, at Spotsylvania, Cold Harbor, and Petersburg. The war became a slugging match, and the armies developed trench warfare tactics. Grant was wearing Lee down, but the Confederacy would not die easily.

Northern photographers, well aware of the marketability of war views after Antietam and Gettysburg, were ever more eager to follow Grant's army. The E. & H. T. Anthony Co. had a number of photographers under contract in Virginia in 1864 and 1865, including operators for Brady, who gave Anthony negatives in exchange for supplies. Brady and his photographers were particularly prolific. An 1864 Brady catalog of photographs of Grant's campaign listed more than 225 views, at a price of fifty cents each. Many were in stereo. Gardner's Gallery also was busy. Gardner advertised that the exposure time for a carte de visite in his studio "rarely exceeds five seconds," adding, "Excellent pictures are on exhibition taken as late in the evening as 6:20." Gardner appointed Timothy O'Sullivan as his director of field operations and dispatched him to the front. O'Sullivan took most of the known Gardner's Gallery war views from 1864.

All of the photographers captured memorable, historic images. But a series of photographs by

O'Sullivan stands out above all. Positioning his stereoscopic camera from an upper floor window of Massaponax Church in Virginia in 1864, O'Sullivan made three 3-D photos of Grant's "Council of War"—a staff meeting between the commander and his generals and staff. O'Sullivan undoubtedly knew that when the candid photos were viewed one after another through the lenses of a stereoscope, the viewer would get the sense that the meeting was proceeding before his eyes. It was realism, a sense of motion, a true feeling of being there.

One or two days before O'Sullivan photographed Grant's meeting, two or more Brady operators found a burial in progress in Fredericksburg and converged on it with two twin-lens stereo cameras and a single-lens, large-plate camera. The evidence that Brady's men had at least two stereo cameras is provided by a unique new stereo view, freshly brought to light, that shows another stereo camera on a tripod in the background.

*A General with his Horse*

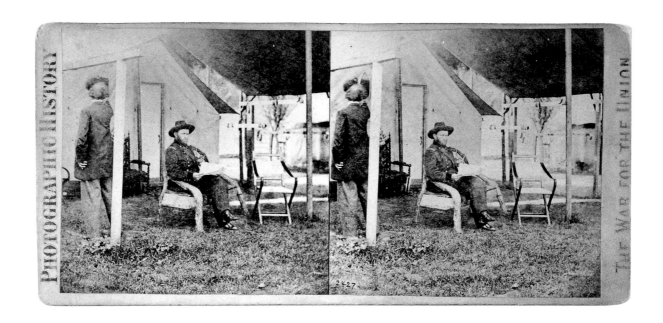

## A SOLDIER WHO FOUGHT

Ulysses Simpson Grant was forty-two years old when these photographs were made near Cold Harbor, Virginia, in June 1864. His unlikely ascension to commander of all the Union armies came ten years after he was compelled to resign from the military in 1854 amid rumors of heavy drinking. He also was a failure in business and farming. But after securing an appointment in 1861, he established a reputation as an officer who fought and won. These images were made by Brady and his operators about three months after Grant was appointed general-in-chief by Lincoln.

756.      Our Boys in the Trenches.
[FOR DESCRIPTION OF THIS VIEW SEE THE OTHER SIDE OF THIS CARD.]

## OUR BOYS IN THE TRENCHES

By 1864, commanders on both sides were inclined to have their troops dig in rather than engage in the outmoded and excessively bloody massed assaults that characterized the early battles of the war. This image by Timothy O'Sullivan shows Union breast-works on the North Anna River on May 25, 1864.

725      Confederate Dead on the Battlefield.
[FOR DESCRIPTION OF THIS VIEW SEE THE OTHER SIDE OF THIS CARD.]

## THE BATTLE NEAR MRS. ALSOP'S HOUSE

On May 20, 1864, near Mrs. Alsop's house at Spotsylvania, O'Sullivan was in the right place at the right time. He photographed dead Confederates lying as they had fallen in an assault the night before. This is the best known of the six photos O'Sullivan took around Mrs. Alsop's house. He used the rifle as a prop, changing its position in different images.

730.

730.     **General Grant's Council of War.**
[FOR DESCRIPTION OF THIS VIEW SEE THE OTHER SIDE OF THIS CARD.]

## GRANT'S COUNCIL OF WAR AT MASSOPONAX CHURCH

On May 21, 1864, one day after his good fortune at Spotsylvania, O'Sullivan scored another coup with his camera. He was present at a staff meeting among Grant and his generals at Massoponax Church, and gained permission to take photographs from the church attic. In the first view, Grant is leaning over the shoulder of Gen. George G. Meade, studying what appears to be a map. In the background, Fifth Corps supply wagons have come to a halt on Telegraph Road, the north-south road that connected Richmond and Fredericksburg. O'Sullivan's second view shows Grant writing a dispatch. He is seated on one of the church pews the officers brought outside. Behind them, the wagon train is moving once again on Telegraph Road. In the third view, Grant is seated directly in front of the two trees. His legs are crossed and he is smoking a cigar. To his left is Assistant Secretary of War Charles A. Dana, and to Dana's left, reading a newspaper, is Gen. John A. Rawlins, Grant's chief of staff.

2508.      Burial of the Dead.

[FOR DESCRIPTION OF THIS VIEW SEE THE OTHER SIDE OF THIS CARD.]

## CREATING A FAMOUS WAR PHOTOGRAPH

Published here for the first time *(above)* is a remarkable image of a Brady & Co. photographer under the hood of a stereo camera mounted on a tripod, preparing to take one of the most notable photographs of the war. The well-known scene captured by the camera *(below)* shows an impromptu burial service, probably staged, in Fredericksburg, Virginia, about May 19, 1864. These Union soldiers most likely fell at Spotsylvania. Using two cameras, Brady operators made at least eight photographs of this scene. This is the first and only known photo of Civil War casualties with a camera in the image.

## THE DESTRUCTION OF CHAMBERSBURG

In July 1864, to ease the pressure on Lee and to avenge Northern destruction in Virginia, Confederates under Gen. Jubal Early invaded Maryland. The Rebels overran Chambersburg, Pennsylvania, on July 30 and threatened to burn the city unless they were paid a ransom of $500,000. When the townspeople declined to pay, the city was torched. Some four hundred buildings and homes were destroyed. The overall view of Chambersburg was part of a series issued by the E. & H. T. Anthony Co. under the sarcastic title "Feats of the Chivalry." In the other view, passers-by gaze at the ruins of the Bank of Chambersburg and the Franklin House.

# THE ART
# OF THE
# STEREO
# PHOTOGRAPHER

120

# Those who seriously study Civil War photography come to realize that many hundreds of war images are, to most modern eyes, static and uninteresting.

They may contain a tremendous amount of valuable information for historians, but many are visually dull. Hundreds of these bland photos were taken for military purposes. An individual James River water battery, for instance, might be photographed from six different angles without anyone in the picture. Even if no one else bought those views, the military did.

But Gardner and Brady, among others, retained a keen sense of the artistic possibilities in their work. In May 1863, Gardner advertised his "Photographic Incidents of the War" as the largest and finest collection of war views ever made. "Apart from the great interest appertaining to them, they stand unequaled as works of art. Amongst the contributors will be found the names of the most distinguished photographers in the country," said Gardner's ad.

Gardner and Brady also took care to present their work, particularly the large-plate photos, in an artistic fashion. Individual eight-by-ten-inch plate prints were mounted on sturdy, high quality, gilt-edged board mounts with printed labels. The mounts were often as large as twenty by twenty-four inches. These prints were $1.50 each, and if a customer bought enough of them, they were bound in a leather-clad cover that was hand-embossed in gold with the title "Incidents of the War." Stereographs also were carefully hand-cropped and mounted. Each had its own printed label.

In 1865 and 1866, Gardner published his elaborate two-volume *Photographic Sketchbook of the War*, which contained one hundred original prints of war scenes. "Verbal representations of such places, or scenes, may or may not have the merit of accuracy; but photographic presentments of them will be accepted by posterity with an undoubting faith," Gardner wrote in a short introduction. "During the four years of war, almost every point of importance has been photographed, and the collection from which these views have been selected amounts to nearly three thousand."

For all of the unexciting photos of the war, photographers left a broad selection of unforgettable images as well. A catalog of Brady's collection of war views said in 1869: "Photography was never before applied to so important an object, and it rarely, if ever, produced such brilliant and satisfactory results."

*Cumberland Landing*
*One hundred thousand men lived in this tent city as the Union Army prepared to march on Richmond.*

## A CAPTAIN AND HIS OFFICERS

This view of Capt. H. H. Pierce and officers of the First Connecticut Heavy Artillery was taken outside Petersburg in 1865.

## ROLLING THE WHITE HOUSE LAWN

Although a war was being fought, certain standards had to be maintained, including the rolling of the White House lawn by top-hatted gardeners.

## THREE REBEL PRISONERS AT GETTYSBURG

This Brady photograph may be the closest in capturing the spirit of the Civil War in the same fashion Joe Rosenthal's image of the Iwo Jima flag raising captured the spirit of World War II. Although Brady and his operators did not arrive at Gettysburg until about two weeks after the battle, they had the good fortune to come upon these prisoners on Seminary Ridge before they were moved out of Gettysburg.

## A LONE GRAVE AT ANTIETAM

At the base of a dead tree in the middle of the Antietam battlefield lies the grave of Pvt. John Marshall, Twenty-eighth Pennsylvania Volunteers, who fell during an assault near the Dunker Church.

## THE BLACK SOLDIER

By 1864, when this photograph was taken near Dutch Gap, thousands of African-Americans had become soldiers. All told, 185,000 blacks served in the Civil War, and more than 38,000 lost their lives.

## THE YOUNGSTERS OF WAR

The caption on this early Anthony war view reads, "Three drummer boys who have been in nine battles of the rebellion."

1214.  Encampment at Cumberland Landing, Va.
[FOR DESCRIPTION OF THIS VIEW SEE THE OTHER SIDE OF THIS CARD.]

## THE ENCAMPMENT AT CUMBERLAND LANDING

Photographer James F. Gibson employed a classic stereo photography technique—combining a vivid foreground element with a panoramic background—in this view of a Union encampment at Cumberland Landing on the Pamunkey River in Virginia during the Peninsular Campaign.

THE WAR FOR THE UNION.

PHOTOGRAPHIC HISTORY.

View taken inside the Petersburg railroad depot,

## THE PETERSBURG RAILROAD DEPOT

Of the many images made amongst the ruins of Richmond at the end of the war, this photograph inside the Petersburg railroad depot stands out as a classic three-dimensional view.

# SHERMAN CAPTURES ATLANTA

# CHAPTER TEN

# When Grant was appointed commander of the Union armies, Maj.

Gen. William Tecumseh Sherman was left in charge of the western theater. On May 6, 1864, Sherman and his army left Chattanooga to march on Atlanta. After a grueling campaign and siege, Atlanta fell on September 1, and Sherman unleashed his March to the Sea, cutting a path of destruction sixty miles wide.

George N. Barnard was one of the country's finest photographers when he joined Sherman on his campaign through Georgia. He had been taking photographs for twenty-one years, initially as a daguerreotype artist. His daguerreotypes of a burning mill in Oswego, New York, in 1853 are considered among the first American news photographs. Early in the war, Barnard worked for Brady.

As Sherman started his campaign, Barnard became official photographer for the Military Division of the Mississippi. Many of the photographs Barnard took on the way to Atlanta were single Imperial images on huge ten-by-fourteen inch glass negatives. But in the hectic days of mid-November 1864, when Atlanta was emptied and burned, Barnard relied on his stereo camera and actually caught a sense of movement and urgency as the soldiers destroyed the railroad.

In February 1865, Sherman captured Columbia, South Carolina. That city burned, too, and Barnard photographed some of the ruins. Ironically, one of the victims was George S. Cook, who had moved his

business and family from beleaguered Charleston to Columbia as a safe haven. Cook's new Columbia gallery burned in the conflagration. Years later, he told descendants that he lost some of his most valuable possessions and much of his work in the final years of the war. Cook and Barnard, who were both born in Connecticut in 1819, did not cross paths in Columbia.

In 1866, Barnard published the elaborate *Photographic Views of Sherman's Campaign*, a large book that included sixty-one contact prints, each ten by fourteen inches. Barnard had added dramatic cloud formations to many of the images by double printing the prints, which were then hand-mounted onto gilt-edged pages. The book cost $150 and, like Gardner's sketchbook, was not very profitable. People were tired of the war. Both books, however, became landmarks in the history of Civil War photography. Today, original prints from dismantled volumes are highly prized by collectors. Still, a typical print sells today for only $300-600, which is comparable to prices paid for twentieth-century Civil War lithographs.

*The Prize of the South*

PHOTOGRAPHIC HISTORY

THE WAR FOR THE UNION.

## SHERMAN BEFORE ATLANTA

Astride his horse in the Rebel defensive works outside Atlanta, Maj. Gen. William Tecumseh
Sherman looks out over the land he conquered.

## PONDER HOUSE

At the end of Peachtree Street, the Confederates
built breastworks in the backyard of the Ponder
House. When the Union Army shelled the posi-
tions, the house was riddled. The home was
misidentified in contemporary captions as the
Potter House.

## WHITEHALL STREET, ATLANTA

On September 2, 1864, after the Confederates withdrew, Sherman occupied Atlanta. He departed on November 16, but only after putting the heart of the city to the torch. Fires raged uncontrolled through Atlanta on the night of November 14, destroying these buildings.

## BEFORE ATLANTA BURNED

In one of the last photographs of Atlanta before it was destroyed, Union Army wagons are poised to begin Sherman's March to the Sea. In the background, a string of boxcars wait to be loaded next to the city's railcar shed.

3671

The last train of cars removing the inhabitants from Atlanta, s 3671.

## LAST TRAIN OUT OF ATLANTA

With baggage piled high on their roofs, these box-cars are ready to leave the city. They were said to be part of the last train removing inhabitants from Atlanta after Sherman ordered its evacuation.

E. & H. T. ANTHONY & CO.,

591 BROADWAY, NEW YORK.

## RUINS OF THE RAILCAR SHED

After the last train left, the massive railcar shed was destroyed. As Sherman departed, he remembered, "Behind us lay Atlanta, smoldering and in ruins, the black smoke rising high in the air, and hanging like a pall...."

## COLUMBIA, SOUTH CAROLINA

After leaving Atlanta and cutting a swath of destruction through Georgia, Sherman's men turned north into South Carolina, where they burned the state capital of Columbia.

# PETERSBURG AND THE FALL OF RICHMOND

# CHAPTER ELEVEN

# While Sherman marched through Georgia, Grant laid siege to Lee's forces at Petersburg, Virginia, just twenty miles south of Richmond. The end was approaching.

Just before Petersburg fell on April 3, 1865, photographer T. C. Roche came in from the field to headquarters at City Point, Virginia, and met with Capt. A. J. Russell, who was a photographer and engineer with the U.S. Military Railroads.

It was a memorable night, as Russell recounted in his remarkable 1882 narrative of their meeting:

"Cap.," said Roche, "I am in for repairs and want to get things ready for the grand move, for the army is sure to move tonight or tomorrow night. The negatives on hand I wish to send North with some letters, prepare my glass and chemicals; in fact, get everything ready for the grand move, for this is the final one, and the Rebellion is broken...."

Roche made his preparations, and then he and Russell "sat smoking and talking of adventures." Russell told the story of the photographer under fire at Dutch Gap.

Suddenly, wrote Russell, "the heavy boom of cannons were heard in the direction of Petersburg. Roche jumped to his feet, and rushing to the door, said, 'Cap., the ball has opened; I must be off....'

"In the next quarter of an hour two horses were harnessed, everything snugly packed, and shaking

*The Mortar "Dictator"*
*Mounted on a small railway car, this thirteen-inch seacoast mortar was the only one of its size used in the siege of Petersburg.*

my hand with a 'we will meet tomorrow at the front,' (Roche) said good bye and the wagon rattled off into the darkness of midnight towards that doomed city, above which was such another display of pyrotechnics as few photos have ever witnessed—shells flying in all directions, leaving their trails of fire and fading away only to be replaced by others. This was not all. The whole world seemed alive; every road was teeming and the call to arms seemed to find a response from every foot of the ground; the rumbling of artillery; the clatter of cavalry, the tramp of infantry, the shrieking of locomotives, calling men to their posts, plainly told that the time had come—that the destiny of a nation hung in the balance."

The next morning, Russell wrote, Petersburg fell. (It was probably the morning of the day after.) Russell found Roche on the ramparts "with scores of negatives taken where the fight had been thickest..."

Roche's photographs of dead Confederate soldiers in Fort Mahone outside Petersburg were the last such images taken during the war. His quick response had given him the opportunity. E. & H. T. Anthony's stereo views of these gruesome scenes undoubtedly sold well, because today these cards are frequently found in collections of war views.

As Petersburg fell, so did Richmond, the capital city of the Confederacy. Fires broke out, some started by looters, others by the fleeing Rebels. Many burned out of control.

On April 4, 1865, President Lincoln toured the ravaged city. He had just eleven days to live. Gardner came back into the field and began making photographs of the destruction of Richmond's commercial district. Brady and his operators also arrived on the scene, as did other photographers.

Not all of the city burned, but an area of several blocks was gutted and became known as the Burnt District. The most distinctive ruin was the remains of Gallego Mills. Some of the best stereo views of the Burnt District are a series of unlabeled views now in the collection of the Virginia Historical Society in Richmond. All that is written on any of the views is a handwritten notation: "Richmond, 1865" and "F. W. Knapp," (possibly the name of the photographer).

### HOW CLOSE THE LINES WERE

Photographer T. C. Roche knew that a good stereo view would enhance the viewer's perception of how close the Union and Rebel lines were at Petersburg. The Confederate breastworks are in the foreground; the mounds of dirt in mid-distance are the Union picket lines.

Entered according to Act of Congress in the year 1865, by E. & H.T. Anthony & Co. in the Clerk's Office of the District Court of the U.S. for the So.District of New York

## A PLACE CALLED "FORT DAMNATION"

This is the Confederate Fort Mahone outside

Petersburg on April 3, 1865, the morning after it was stormed by Union troops. They had to run through its trenches and fight in its mud. They called it "Fort Damnation."

951.    First Wagon Train Entering Petersburg.

[FOR DESCRIPTION OF THIS VIEW SEE THE OTHER SIDE OF THIS CARD.]

## OCCUPIED PETERSBURG

Although the caption of this photo says it shows the first wagon train entering the conquered city,

photohistorian William A. Frassanito has determined that this long line of wagons was actually leaving Petersburg. The photo was probably taken by John Reekie about a week after the city fell.

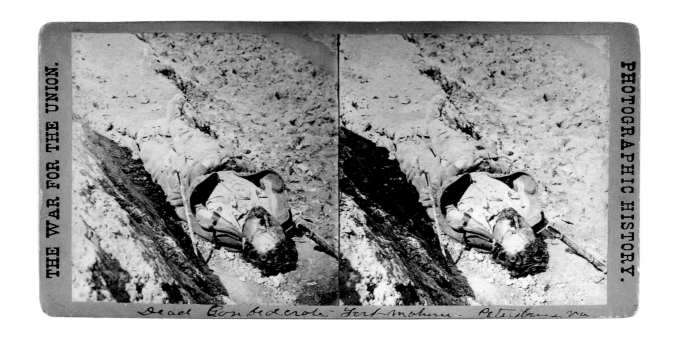

### AMONG THE LAST TO FALL

Six days before Lee surrendered at Appomattox, Roche took these photographs of the dead Confederates who had defended Petersburg. He exposed twenty-two negatives of the human wreckage. It was the last series of death studies made during the war.

### A HOME THAT GOT IN THE WAY

The great bombardment that sent Roche rushing to the front with his cameras had its effect on the civilian population of Petersburg. Many homes were damaged, and several shells crashed into the east parlor of the Dunlop House.

### REBELS CAPTURED BY SHERIDAN

Prisoners were taken by the hundreds in the war's final days. After photographing Fort Mahone outside Petersburg on April 3, Roche found these Confederates, on their way to the rear after being captured at Five Forks by the troops of Gen. Philip Sheridan.

## THE FALL OF RICHMOND

As they evacuated Richmond on April 2, the Confederates spared the capitol building, but burned a large section of the city. Proper ladies of the city found cause to don their mourning dresses, not only for the city but for the Confederacy as well. For years afterward, this section was known as the Burnt District, even though it was soon rebuilt.

**GALLEGO MILLS**

Gallego Mills was one of the most imposing structures in Richmond during the war. After its destruction, it was the city's most spectacular ruin.

# THE END
# OF
# THE WAR

# CHAPTER TWELVE

# After the war ended with Lee's surrender on April 9, 1865, the photographers were met with a legion of photographic opportunities.

On April 14, Old Glory was raised once again at Fort Sumter by its former commander, Robert Anderson, who was now a general. E. & H. T. Anthony Co. photographers were there, as was George S. Cook. That night, Lincoln was assassinated in Washington and soon after Gardner photographed Ford's Theater. In Richmond, Brady sought out Lee the day after he returned to the city and on April 15 captured perhaps the greatest series of Lee photos. On April 27, Gardner photographed the dramatic autopsy on the body of John Wilkes Booth. The image has never surfaced, reportedly because Secretary of War Edwin Stanton ordered the negative and print destroyed to prevent profiteering.

On May 24 and 25, the Grand Review of the Armies paraded through Washington and the victorious spectacle was recorded by the stereo camera. The Lincoln conspirators were executed on July 7, and Andersonville's notorious commander, Henry Wirz, was hung from a hangman's noose on November 10. Both executions were extensively photographed by Gardner, who used several cameras, both stereo and single lens. But at the key moment in the hanging of the Lincoln conspirators Gardner used his stereo camera.

These hangings were the final great photographic events of the Civil War. In the years afterward, Gardner and O'Sullivan became pioneering photographers in the American West. In 1869, O'Sullivan carried his camera deep into the silver mines of

*To Those Who Fell*
*This garland-draped cross was one of the early postwar memorials in Arlington Cemetery.*

Virginia City, Nevada, and ignited piles of magnesium to illuminate scenes of working miners. Brady, meanwhile, spent most of the rest of his life mired in financial trouble. Barnard lost his photo gallery in the Chicago fire of 1871 but carried on, making photographs well into the 1880s. Roche continued to work for E. & H. T. Anthony Co. and received a number of patents for his photographic inventions. And Cook, the first combat photographer, remained in Charleston until 1880, when he moved to Richmond and opened a gallery. After an illustrious career, he died in 1902.

For all of these men, and most of their generation, nothing ever equaled their experiences from 1861 to 1865. In their zeal to capture the war with their cameras, these pioneers of photo journalism, both North and South, had achieved important photographic milestones and created an unparalleled visual record of the greatest conflict in our history.

Entered according to Act of Congress, in the year 1862, by Gardner & Gibson, in the Clerk's Office of the District Court of the District of Columbia.

McLEAN HOUSE, APPOMATTOX C. H., VA.　　By A. H. PLECKER, Lynchburg, Va.

## THE TWO HOUSES OF WILMER McLEAN

At the beginning of the Civil War, Wilmer McLean's house was stuck in the thick of the war. Confederate Gen. P. G. T. Beauregard used it as a headquarters during the first battle of Bull Run.

McLean vowed to move his family to a place where the war wouldn't find them. He found a home at Appomattox Court House deep in central Virginia and lived there peacefully until April 9, 1865, when Lee surrendered to Grant in McLean's parlor. Souvenir-hungry officers promptly scoured his house for keepsakes.

## A SILENT ARSENAL

Captured siege guns were lined up wheel to wheel in Richmond. Their days of belching shells were over. Many would end up in city parks or on the national battlefield parks established in the late nineteenth and early twentieth centuries.

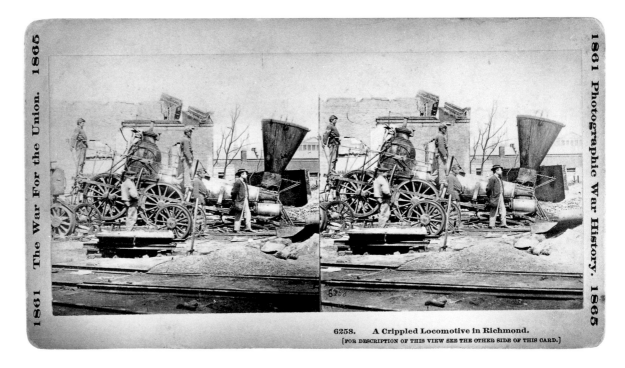

6258. A Crippled Locomotive in Richmond.
[FOR DESCRIPTION OF THIS VIEW SEE THE OTHER SIDE OF THIS CARD.]

## THE CONFEDERATE RAILROAD

The reunited United States now entered the period of our history called Reconstruction, and for railroads, factories, and businesses all across the South, that reconstruction was literal.

3404. Place where President Lincoln was Assassinated.
[FOR DESCRIPTION OF THIS VIEW SEE THE OTHER SIDE OF THIS CARD.]

## LINCOLN'S BOX AT FORD'S THEATER

Lee surrendered to Grant at Appomattox Court House, Virginia, on April 9, 1865. On April 14, the Union flag was ceremoniously raised at Fort Sumter. That night, President and Mrs. Lincoln went to Ford's Theater to see *Our American Cousin*. While sitting in the box to the right, Linclon was fatally wounded by a shot from the derringer of actor John Wilkes Booth, who dislodged the stars and stripes bunting with his spur while jumping from the box to make his escape across the stage. Alexander Gardner made this photo soon after the assassination, while Lincoln's rocking chair was still in the box.

## LINCOLN'S FUNERAL IN COLUMBUS, OHIO

This Lincoln funeral photograph is published here for the first time in its entirety, showing Lincoln's casket being borne into the state-house at Columbus. The pallbearers have removed the casket from the bier, and are carrying it toward the state capitol building, which is to the left of the photo. After leaving Washington, it took twenty days for the president's body to reach Springfield, Illinois, with stops at all the places where Lincoln stopped on his way to the capital in 1861.

Entered according to act of Congress in the year 1865, by A. GARDNER, in the Clerk's Office of the District Court for the District of Columbia.

## SIC SEMPER SICARIIS

The Latin phrase means "always thus for assassins," and thus it was for four of the conspirators in Lincoln's assassination. They were tried in Washington and hanged on July 7, 1865. Alexander Gardner had three cameras trained on the scaffold and took at least a dozen photos of the execution. But he reserved the key moment—"The Drop"—for his stereo camera. Left to right are Mary Surratt, the first woman executed in the United States, Lewis Payne, David Herold, and George Atzerodt.

## THE GRAND REVIEW

For the North, there was one last spasm of celebration—The Grand Review of the Armies down Pennsylvania Avenue. It took two days, May 24 and 25, and was extensively photographed. On the left is the Willard Hotel, Washington's most prestigious hostelry during the war and a landmark for more than 130 years.

## ARLINGTON CEMETERY

The government turned the grounds of Lee's old estate in Arlington into a military cemetery that soon became the nation's most famous burial ground.

Apple Vender. — Boston Common.

## PATRONIZE THE DISABLED SOLDIER

The war changed the future for thousands of young men. Many were disabled and suffered pain from their wounds for the rest of their lives. In Boston Common, these two veterans—one legless and the other apparently missing an arm—solicit funds by selling candy and lemonade.

# BIBLIOGRAPHY

At the foundation of the modern study of Civil War photographs are four books by William A. Frassanito: *Gettysburg: A Journey in Time*. New York: Charles Scribner's Sons, 1975; *Antietam: The Photographic Legacy of America's Bloodiest Day*. New York: Charles Scribner's Sons, 1978; *Grant and Lee: The Virginia Campaigns 1864-1865*. New York: Charles Scribner's Sons, 1983; and *Early Photography at Gettysburg*. Gettysburg, Pennsylvania: Thomas Publications, 1995.

The two most comprehensive photographic histories of the war are the six-volume *The Image of War*, William C. Davis, Editor. Garden City, New York: Doubleday & Company, 1981-1984 and *The Photographic History of the Civil War in Ten Volumes*, Francis Trevelyan Miller, Editor in Chief. New York: The Review of Reviews Co., 1911. Neither, however, reproduces any stereo views.

The best modern guide to stereo views is *Stereo Views: An Illustrated History and Price Guide*, by John Waldsmith. Radnor, Pennsylvania: Wallace-Homestead Book Company, 1991.

The finest study of the photographs of Abraham Lincoln is *Lincoln in Photographs: An Album of Every Known Pose*, by Charles Hamilton and Lloyd Ostendorf. Dayton, Ohio: Morningside House, 1985.

The best biography of M. B. Brady is *Mathew Brady and His World*, by Dorothy Meserve Kunhardt and Philip B. Kunhardt Jr. Alexandria, Virginia: Time-Life Books, 1977. The only biography of Alexander Gardner is the lavish *Witness to an Era: The Life and Photographs of Alexander Gardner*, by D. Mark Katz. New York: Viking, 1991. There is also the excellent *George N. Barnard, Photographer of Sherman's Campaign*, by Keith F. Davis. Kansas City: Hallmark Cards, Inc., 1990.

Author Jack C. Ramsay, Jr., a great grandson of George S. Cook, has published a thousand-edition biography of his ancestor, called *Photographer Under Fire*. Minneapolis, Minnesota: Bolger Publications, 1994.

Dover Publications, Inc., of New York, New York, has produced paperback reprint editions of Gardner's *Photographic Sketchbook of the War* (1959); *Photographic Views of Sherman's Campaign* by George N. Barnard (1977); and a volume of images by A. J. Russell called *Russell's Civil War Photographs* (1982).

## NSA

The National Stereoscopic Association is a non-profit organization that encourages and promotes the study and collection of stereoscopic images. It publishes *Stereo World* six times a year and conducts an annual convention with a trade fair and auction. For membership information, write the association at P.O. Box 14801, Columbus, Ohio 43214.

# INDEX

## A

Action photography, 17, 65–73
African Americans, 28–29, 94
Ambrotypes, 15
Amputations, 76
Anderson, Gen. Robert, 21, 111
Andersonville, Georgia, 75
Anthony, Edward, 16
Anthony Co. (E. and H. T.), 54, 57, 83, 89, 103, 111
Antietam, battle of, 17, 37–45, 69, 93
Appomattox Court House, 112, 114
Arlington Cemetery, 111, 116
Atlanta, 73, 97–100
Atzerodt, George, 115

## B

Barnard, George, 16, 27, 73, 97, 111
Beauregard, Gen. P. G. T., 112
Berger, Anthony, 51, 52
Booth, John Wilkes, 15, 111, 114
Boston, 117
Boston Light Artillery, 31
Brady, M. B.
   artistic sense of, 91
   birth of, 9
   effect of photographs of, 75
   first name of, 9
   Lincoln photographs of, 50, 52
   photographers working for, 16–17
   photograph of, 13
   in the first year of the war, 17, 27
   at Antietam, 40
   at Gettysburg, 57, 62–63, 93
   Grant's campaign and, 83, 84, 88
   at Richmond, 104, 111
   after the war, 111
Brewster, David, 16
Brown, John, 29
Bull Run
   first battle, 17, 27, 32, 112
   second battle, 37
Burns, John L., 57, 63
Burnside, Maj. Gen. Ambrose E., 13
Burnside's Bridge, 37, 44

## C

Centreville, Virginia, 32
Chambersburg, Pennsylvania, 89
Cold Harbor, Virginia, 13, 77, 83
Columbia, South Carolina, 97, 101
Columbus, Ohio, 114
Cook, George S., 17, 21, 65–67, 75, 97, 111
Cook's Battery, 31
Cooley, Sam, 9
Culpeper, Virginia, 70
Cumberland Landing, Virginia, 95
Custer, Lt. George Armstrong, 33

## D

Daguerre, Louis Jacques Mande, 14
Daguerreotypes, 14–15
Dana, Charles A., 86
Doubleday, Capt. Abner, 25
Drummer boys, 81, 94
Dunkers, 40
Dunlop House, 107
Durbec, F. E., 21, 22, 24
Dutch Gap Canal, 65, 68

## E

Early, Gen. Jubal, 89
Ellsworth, Col. Elmer, 30
Elmira, New York, 75, 79
Embalming, 77
Essex, Camp, 31

## F

Fair Oaks, battle of, 33, 69
Ford's Theater, 15, 111, 114
Franklin House, 89
Frassanito, William A., 9, 57, 58, 105
Fredericksburg, Virginia, 76, 83, 88

## G

Gaines's Mill, 27, 34
Gallego Mills, 104, 109
Gardner, Alexander
   artistic sense of, 91
   Brady and, 16–18
   Lincoln photographs of, 45, 50, 53, 54
   slavery photographs of, 29
   in the first year of the war, 27
   at Antietam, 17, 37–39, 41–42, 45, 69
   at Gettysburg, 57–61
   Grant's campaign and, 76, 83
   at Richmond, 104
   Lincoln assassination and, 114, 115
   after the war, 111
Gettysburg, battle of, 17, 57–63, 91, 93
Gibson, James F., 17, 27, 34, 37–38, 57, 78, 95
Grand Review of the Armies, 111, 116
Grant, Gen. Ulysses S., 83–84, 86–87, 103, 112, 114
Gutekunst, Frederick, 11

## H

Hampton, Wade, 22
Harper's Ferry, Virginia, 29
Herold, David, 115
Holmes, Oliver Wendell, 14, 38
Hood, Gen. John Bell, 72
Houston, F. K., 21

## I

*Ironsides*, 65–67

## J

James River, 78

**K**

Keene, Laura, 15

**L**

Lamon, Ward Hill, 45
Larkin, J. E., 79
Lee, Gen. Robert E., 29, 37, 57, 83, 103, 111, 112, 114, 116
Le Mere, Thomas, 50
Libby Prison, 79
Lincoln, Abraham
    photographs of, 16, 47–55
    first inauguration of, 49
    at Antietam, 45
    places Grant in command, 83
    second inauguration of, 53
    at Richmond, 104
    assassination of, 15, 55, 111, 114–15
    funeral of, 114
Lincoln, Tad, 52
Lookout Valley, Tennessee, 72
Louisiana Historical Association Collection, 21
Lowell, Massachusetts, 30
Lutheran Theological Seminary, 63

**M**

Mahone, Fort, 103, 105, 107
Manassas, Virginia, 27
Marshall House, 30
Massoponax Church, 83, 86
McClellan, Gen. George B., 27, 33, 37, 45, 69
McLean, Wilmer, 112
Meade, Gen. George C., 59, 86
Meigs, Brig. Gen. Montgomery C., 49
*Monitor*, 78
Morris Island, 21, 24
Moultrie, Fort, 21, 23, 25, 66, 67

**N**

Nashville, battle of, 72
New York Zouaves, 30, 76
North Anna River, 73, 85

**O**

Onandaga, 78
Osborn, James M., 21, 22, 24
Ostendorf, Lloyd, 47, 48, 50, 52, 53
O'Sullivan, Timothy
    Brady and, 16
    George S. Cook and, 67
    in the first year of the war, 27, 35
    at Gettysburg, 57
    Grant's campaign and, 73, 83, 85, 86
    after the war, 111

**P**

Pamunkey River, 95
Payne, Lewis, 115
Petersburg, Virginia, 92, 95, 103–7

Photography, history of, 14–16
Pickens, Francis, 22
Pickett's Charge, 59, 62
Ponder House, 98
Pope, Gen. John, 37
Prisons, 75, 79

**R**

Rappahannock River, 35
Rawlins, Gen. John A., 86
Reekie, John, 105
Richmond, 79, 104, 108–9, 111, 113
Roche, T. C., 68, 103, 104, 106–7, 111
Russell, A. J., 68, 70, 103

**S**

San Francisco, 13
Savage Station, 17, 27, 34
Sheridan, Gen. Philip, 107
Sherman, Maj. Gen. William Tecumseh, 73, 97–101
Ships, 67, 78, 80
Slavery, 28–29, 35
Soule, John P., 9
Spotsylvania, Virginia, 85, 88
Springfield, Illinois, 55, 114
Stanton, Edwin, 111
Stereo photography
    art of, 91–95
    cameras for, 17
    history of, 16
    popularity of, 13–14, 18–19
Sullivan's Island, 21, 22, 25
Sumter, Fort, 9, 16, 21–25, 65–67, 111, 114
Surratt, Mary, 115

**T**

Taylor and Huntington views, 18–19
Thomas, Gen. George, 72
Tintypes, 15
Tipton, W. H., 19
Townsend, George Alfred, 9, 16, 27
Trapier Mortar Battery, 24

**V**

Vance, Robert H., 14
Vicksburg, Mississippi, 80, 83

**W**

Walker, Lewis E., 48
Washington, Lt. J. B., 33
*Weehawken*, 66, 67
Wheatstone, Charles, 16
White House, 92
Willard Hotel, 116
Wirz, Henry, 111

**Y**

Yorktown, Virginia, 33

24

*Photograph Dept*

PHOTOGRAPHED BY THE

# AMERICAN STEREOSCOPIC COMPANY,

*W. LANGENHEIM, General Agent,*

722 Chestnut St., Philad'a.

NEGATIVES TAKEN BY A. WATSON.

---

1861     **THE WAR FOR THE UNION.**     1865

### PHOTOGRAPHIC HISTORY.

This series of pictures are *original photographs* taken during the war of the Rebellion. A quarter of a century has passed away since the sun painted these real scenes of the great war, and the "negatives" have undergone chemical changes which makes it slow and difficult work to get "prints" from them. Of course no more "negatives" can be made, as the scenes represented by this series of war views have passed away forever. The great value of these pictures is apparent. Some "negatives" are entirely past printing from, and all of them are very slow printers.

### A WORD AS TO PRICES.

A gentleman living near Watkins' Glen, New York, wrote us that he thought twenty-five cents each, too high a price for the stereoscopic war views, as he could buy views of Watkins' Glen for $1.50 per dozen. We wrote him to this effect; if there was but one negative of Watkins' Glen in existence, and if Watkins' Glen itself was entirely wiped off the face of the earth, and if this one negative was old and "dense" and very slow to "print," and if all the people of this country were as much interested in a view of Watkins' Glen as they are in seeing the real scenes of our great war, so faithfully reproduced, *then*, and *only under such circumstances*, should Watkins' Glen Pictures be compared to photographs made "at the front" during the days of 1861 to 1865. The gentleman "acknowledged the corn," took the war views he wished for, paid the reasonable price asked for them, and was satisfied.

The above is the only answer we shall ever make to the question of *price*. We deem it necessary to say this much, as many persons write and ask us for *cheap* war views; when we change the price of these war views, it will be to double it; they will never be any cheaper than now. They can be obtained only of

*Copyrighted.*     TAYLOR & HUNTINGTON, Publishers, No. 2 State Street, HARTFORD, CONN.

---

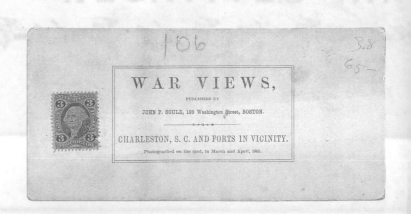

WAR VIEWS,

PUBLISHED BY

JOHN P. SOULE, 199 Washington Street, BOSTON.

CHARLESTON, S. C. AND FORTS IN VICINITY.

Photographed on the spot, in March and April, 1865.